MW00875384

Chasing Blackbeard
The Carolina Series

By Steven Davis

Illustrated by Ann-Catherine Davis

Modelling Provided By Elizabeth "Lizzy" Ellis

* * * * * * * * *

Sovereign Tomorrow Publications

Special Thanks

I would like to offer a very special Thank You to Danny "Fuzzy" Ferrell for offering help with the research going into this book. Not only did he share his vast knowledge of Blackbeard but also brought forth some great literature that only made this journey more enjoyable.

Thank You to the incredible people of Bath North Carolina for always being so friendly to those from the outside that are constantly visiting your beautiful little town in search for an essence and feel of times long lost to the rest of the world.

Thank You to the people of Ocracoke Island for quite possibly having the most beautiful and serene beaches in the world. One visit to your quaint little world would inspire anyone and it' the very reason that I will continue to court you for the rest of my life.

Beaufort and the people there of have always shared a very special affection for Blackbeard, and he had that same affection for you. His love affair with you made you the perfect place for The North Carolina Maritime Museum. This museum is a great place to enjoy for people of all ages.

My Story

I am here to tell you my story. To be honest, I am actually here to tell you his story. And of him, much you will read. But first, I need you to know who I am, where I am from, what I did and why I did it.

I am Eli Ellis. I am writing this final entry in the year of 1783 in The Year Of Our Lord. There is nothing left to me but skin and bones. I am but only an old fool now. I live a simple life here in Bath Towne or as simple as possible. In this day and time, things are simply more complicated. Things are more controlled. It appears that we are to be the new nation of America. Should it be strangulation by Congress or Crown, it is still strangulation. I do not know when this journal will be found; or if it will. Should it be, that still offers no promise of appreciation. But in doing so, I have fulfilled my obligations.

Again, I am Eli Ellis. I was born in the year 1702 here in Bath. It has been Bath Towne for as long as I can remember. Our little home here on the water became a town when I was just knee high. It was 1705, but I remember it still. It is one of my first memories. The celebration was huge. We became recognized and official. As you know, all things must be official. There were fireworks and explosions across the water. Albeit beautiful, it is what I imagine the end of the world will look like. Pray tell, I will not be around to see it.

When I look back on the early days of this town, I question how we ever made it. Things were much tougher then. Things are given to people these days. Everything is convenient. This generation will never know survival in its truest form.

At our foundation were many French Huguenots. They were Protestant reformers that only sought to live a simple life. As a child, I can remember there being a small church just west of the port, a sawmill, and over a dozen houses. There were two pubs and several boarding houses amongst our sprawl. Records show that there were about 60 of us. With the winds of a storm, that number could become 300. That port was a doorway to a world far bigger than any of us could grasp. The Port Of Bath was both The Pearly Gates as well as The Gates Of Hell. If this town stands another 80 years, it will be due to that doorway and if we collapse and burn tomorrow; that too will be at its hands. There is no method of determination that will share what will come through next. It is where I once met The Devil Himself.

By the time I had seen 15 years, we had survived attacks from The Tuscarora, multiple epidemics including Yellow Fever, a severe drought, and a dastardly political war that became known as Cary's Rebellion.

The Tuscarora constantly pushed back on the intrusion of British, Dutch, and German settlers. Fearful of their strength, numbers, and constant barbarism, they enlisted the help of The Yamasee and The Cherokee. The bloodshed was enough to cripple our small settlement, but we were strong. We were to be the first capital of the colony. I truly believe that The Tuscarora would have fought on forever. Then, something came from the port that brought more unchallenged power and savagery than even they understood. Eventually, they abandoned all ideas of reclaiming that land. It belonged to the sea and demons came from the sea.

When Yellow Fever swept through, all hope was lost. There may have been dozens of us, but those dozens could have easily become nothing when such a thing arrives. We were all aware of the stories and happenings to other settlements. There is no fighting it. Its origination most likely came through that damn port. With it either being the world or God righting itself, the medications needed to treat the suffering would also pass through its gates.

When the drought fell upon us, the fields were barren. No amount of hard work or labor would fix our quandary. The port would tease us with an abundance of water and yet; it was too salty to use. It would kill our plants. Still, though, food from neighboring settlements would eventually come. And through that port is where it entered.

Cary's Rebellion was a bloody battle between The Quakers and The Church of England. It was fought right here on these very lands over the governorship of what was at the time, The whole Carolina province. It once stretched from the Spanish lands in Florida all the way to Virginia. But it wasn't the title that was so close to their hearts. It was that port. That port brought in a sewer of corrupt money for the one that controlled it. It was the cause of our strife. Once again, it would right its own wrongs by allowing The Royal Marines of Governor Spottswood to pour in. He had sent these forces from Virginia. They would quickly, yet harshly put the fighting to bed.

As I said, these things were all witnessed before I was the age of 15. And at 15, I saw something far more awesome. There was something vastly more powerful that would come from the sea. No storm or swell of water could ever invade a place as "they" could. Our discussion has moved now from history; to pirates.

Little did I know at the time, I was living in what would eventually become known as The Golden Age Of Piracy. Do pirates still exist in a time when The British rule the seas? Yes. Of course, they do. I assume that they always will. But no time will ever offer the names that I grew up reading about. Not a gazette to be found would be without the names of Anne Bonny, William Kidd, Calico Jack, Mary Read, Henry Every, Sam Bellamy, Henry Morgan, and Benjamin Hornigold. While I adored them all in literature, Horigold was by far my favorite. I loved all of his tales and the way that he was written about. I wanted to do this. I could read and write very well and could think of nothing else other than to share my own stories of piracy. My dilemma came in that I had no stories and I personally knew no pirates. This would change all too soon.

The pub that sat just from the mouth of The Port of Bath was an alluring bait to me. I knew that pirates would stop there with normalcy. Ferrell's Tavern was owned and operated by the brothers, Daniel and John Ferrell. No matter the gap in local customers, their pockets were instantly filled with booty from other lands as soon as I saw those ominous sales in the moonlight.

Their flags would clap and call to me in the salty air. I had been forbidden from even thinking about going within its proximity.

The Port of Bath was everything a pirate wanted when away from the sea. It gave them cover from the sea and those that would hunt them. The broken Carolina coastline was a paint splatter of islands, inlets, and hideouts. Our particular nest also gave them access to our governor. Governor Charles Eden was an installed fixture that coveted the pirate lifestyle. He not only allowed it but encouraged it. Many pirates secretly worked under him or would share a portion of their reapings in trade for allowing them to continue in his waters.

The people of Bath were a swell of emotions when it came to the subject. Pirates were an unsightly sore on us and the new world. They disrupted commerce. They were murderers and rapists. Moreso, they could be sadists and terrorists depending on the name in which we speak. But let us not forget that when the seas would wash them up into the Pamlicoe River, with them came silver and gold. We would also see fresh linens, spices, medications, and supplies. They were an instant connection to lands that most of us would never see.

I haven't tears enough for how badly I hurt and yearn to go in when I see that they have arrived. If to only sit and watch. To hear their stories; to find how they interact with each other. They walked and lived as gods while worshippers like myself would trade a lifetime for an hour of their normalcy.

I punish myself with the fantasy. Hidden under the third floorboard from the window were a stack of pamphlets and journals about them. If left out, my mother would have instantly used them to light the stove.

Then, March the 2nd, 1717 occurred. I had gone for a walk. No matter the fact that this walk randomly took me pass the port. This was of pure coincidence should anyone question. At the age of 15, one could be a farmer, a sailor, a husband or wife. I could certainly take a walk with my dog.

I neared Ferrell's and I could smell the beautiful smoke in the air. It was a blend of the many things that they were smoking in their pipes, cigars, etc. I could hear their laughter, loud talking, and spirited music. The lanterns hung outside and flirted with me; offering me silhouettes.

On the road, the dog and I came across a hat. It was most certainly one of theirs. How it made it to the road, I could only imagine. I suppose the wind may have brought it. Maybe it had been dropped in a drunken stagger. Another dog other than my own may have found it interesting for a bit. But of all these; I like to think it was fate. My parents expected me home and so I would obey their wishes. But if the pirates were still there tomorrow, I had a duty to return it. Then, I looked upward to see the flag. It was Hornigold. Pirates would typically be there for days once docked. Nothing would keep me from meeting him. I would show up tomorrow and be the strapping young man that any crew would desire. Eli Ellis would meet and mingle with the gods.

****

I slept with that hat. I awoke with that hat. I could only imagine the array of things that it had seen. From England to Hispaniola, I knew that it had seen Kraken and mermaid alike.

I slowly snuck into my younger brother's room. Only about six months earlier, he had been gifted a brand new suit. He was always getting new clothing it seemed. Not I. He grew like a weed and had now caught up with me despite there being more than two years between us. I was small and the scrawny sort. His shoulders were starting to widen. His voice had started to deepen. There was no doubt that he would soon be using father's razor and strap. This was in no way the story for myself though. No, Eli Ellis was barely more than a sack of flour and truly had no business trying to move one either. A sack of flour could best me without a doubt.

I must admit, I was quite happy with myself. I was adorned with nicely polished shoes. My hair was in a tight braid as any gentleman would have when trying to force an impression. The suit fit me better than I expected other than I did not have the shoulders for it. No matter. Captain Hornigold was not seeking perfection. I was sure he simply wanted a hard worker.

I quietly closed the front door and walked out on the porch. As I leaned over our railing, my imagination instantly transported me to the ship. I peered over the edge and the water would occasionally spray in my face. I loved it. Seagulls swept over our heads. The wind was behind us in perfect fashion for travel. We would make good time today. If only, it were not just a front porch in a port town.

I walked fast and was upon Ferrell's Tavern in no time. Once again, there was laughter and there was yelling. The air outside was hung heavy with exotic smoke in which one could not imagine the origins. Again, I could hear music that was unlike anything I had ever heard. The lanterns were lit and I could only reckon that this may be the most lively spot on the planet right now.

I straightened my lapel and pulled my shirt sleeves toward my wrists so that they properly flowed from my jacket. I have studied the outfits of pirates for years. I knew that they were sharp dressers from every artist's rendition. They were men of wealth and power. Fine threads were nothing to them. I had to impress from their very first memory of me. I needed to appear worldly and educated if I were to convince them of my value.

I looked into the port. There was now another ship docked. Pirates were drawn to Bath and always would be. The second ship was just as impressive as that of Captain Hornigold and perhaps even more awe-inspiring. It was the ship of female pirates, Ambera McDaniels and Anne-Catherine Davies. They were rumored to have run a tight ship as co-captains and were very respected at sea. This became truer as they obviously were here tonight, side by side with that of Hornigold's men.

I was glad that they were there because if things did not go well with Hornigold for any reason, I had another option. As bad as I would love to spend years by the side of the fabled captain of my admirations, I wanted to be at sea regardless and if they needed more help on their boat, I would gladly answer to Ambera and Anne-Catherine for opportunities to see the world through a pirate's eye.

I slowly walked closer. I have no reason to be dishonest. I was very nervous. I knew that others had been allowed on board at 15, but I did not feel overly impressive.

As I neared the door, I heard something coming from between the tavern and the smokehouse. There was a narrow alley there and it was the source of the ruckus that had caught my attention. As I walked by, I stopped and turned. My jaw hit the ground.

There was a naked lady there facing me. Her rear was in the air and her hands were on the ground in front of her acting as braces. Her hair fell over her head. Behind her was a large, bald, shirtless man with his hands on her hips. He was looking up into the night sky and grinding himself into her with conviction. As she moaned, he would grunt. There it was; I had seen two people have carnal relations for the first time. I was frozen.

After an eternal five or six seconds, he looked down to see me caught in my gaze. He smiled. "Wait your turn, lad. I won't be long. Now get on your way."

She quickly lifted one hand and pulled her hair back. She looked up to make eye contact with me also and spoke in a motherly voice. "You can stay right there. Get your coin ready. I can make sure he's done whenever I'm ready."

I was a statue; a worthless, petrified statue. Another second or two passed and I finally broke the trance. I quickly made my way to the deck. There were men drinking everywhere and women hanging all over them. None of these men looked familiar to me obviously; as they were not from here. But the women did not look familiar either. I suppose they were brought along as supplies.

As I made my way through the crowd, I hung my head low. I did not want to be recognized or draw attention. The smoke was heavy and I was submerged in it. This was not tobacco or at least not any that I had ever known. By the time that I reached the door, my thinking was a slight bit distorted and my vision was double what it should be. I only found the doorknob on my second attempt.

The large room was alive and it was a creature that I had never seen. While I doubt that John or Daniel Ferrell would recognize or even know my name, I did avoid the bar area to add extra caution. I went the other direction completely. There were no two men more fit to handle a large and unruly crowd such as this. Both had served in the Spanish Armada, had been highwaymen through Appalachia and had even served with pirate crews. They had the respect of everyone in the room. I was of little concern to them.

As I waded to the corner booth, I saw the two infamous vixens and instantly knew who they were. I was more than interested in the seating arrangements that they had chosen. Despite the fact that there were extra chairs, Ambera was sitting on the lap of Anne-Catherine. I found it odd. I tried to watch without staring.

Both were laughing and talking to several others that were sitting around. Ambera lifted the colorful, ceramic pipe from the table and struck a match. As she pulled hard to fill her lungs, the match sunk down into the end of it and smoke billowed everywhere. After holding the deep breath in for a moment, she turned to Anne-Catherine and gently pulled her mouth open with her finger and blew the smoke into her mouth. Anne-Catherine closed her eyes and held the gift inside. Finally, she released it and smiled. As the two looked at each other, they slowly kissed. I had found Gomorrah in which Genesis had warned of.

"Are you lost?" Ambera barked at me. I realized that I was once more staring. "Have you never seen two people in love?"

I knew I could not appear shy. I smiled and went immediately to the seat by their side.

"No, not lost at all. My apologies for the gaze. I was taken by the beauty in which you both displayed and I absolutely adore the fact that you are open with your love. There are no judgements on my part."

Anne-Catherine looked at me. "I should hope not. This is no place to seek trouble. We do not wander into your town and we expect none of your ways or rules to come here."

"No, No ma'am. None of that. I am actually here to proposition you. This life here has nothing for me. I seek to join you on the sea."

"Join us? Why would we need you? You have something to offer that my crew cannot already fulfill?"

"Well yes, I do. I have much to offer, in fact!"

"You do? So have experience in careening a ship?"

"Well no . . ."

"You have experience in tar and oil coating?"

"I do not." I hung my head.

"You are an expert with the compass? Reading the sun? You are a rope weaver?"

"No. No, ma'am. I am none of those."

"Then I must ask, silly lad . . . what is it you offer to us?"

"Well, I am a scribe."

"A scribe?" Anne-Catherine drew from her pipe once more.

"Yes. I am a scribe. I want to document your plight. I want to write to the world so that they know of your journey. I can also handle all letters, documents and forms you may encounter or need sending."

"Let me ask you a question, boy. Why would I want the world to know what it is that we do? We come to small, hidden ports such as this one to avoid others being in our business. We do not require your services."

"But . . ."

"No. You seem like a strapping lad but . . . "

Ambera cut in over Anne-Catherine in laughter. "You refer to him as strapping" He is no more than 12."

"I am 15!" I quickly calmed my tone. "I am 15. If you allow me to travel with you, I will cause you no harm and will stay out of the way."

"And you will not eat? Food, water, and resources are a prized possession the moment land fades in the distance. You will only be a dead weight to us. I offer you my apologies. We will speak with you on this more in a few years."

I stood up and smiled politely. I bowed and showed thanks. "Ladies, I hope you have a great evening. I in no way meant to pester."

"You were no problem. We wish you luck. By the way, you are without a drink. Why?"

"Honestly? I am avoiding the bar. I do not wish the owners to see me here."

"Ahhhhhh, I understand. Take my bottle of rum. This will relax you and you will seem a better fit here."

"Thank you again, ladies. Thank you very much."

"Go speak with Hornigold. He has a much larger crew and more than one ship. He also has regular dealings with many in government. Perhaps he will need your services more so than we."

"I will. Have you seen him?" I was suddenly covered in excitement that could not be hidden.

"That is he in the other corner. He has the red lapels."

"Thank you! I did not recognize him instantly from the others. You two, on the other hand, stood out like flowers in the desert."

Anne-Catherine slowly ran her hand between Ambera's thighs in clear view to all. "Did you hear that? We are flowers in the desert." Once more, they began to kiss.

I stood for a moment to clear my thoughts. I was still affected by the smoke that hung so heavily and now, I was holding a bottle of rum. Looking around the room, I was the only one not drinking. Even the Ferrell brothers were pouring shot after shot. Eli Ellis would no longer be a sore thumb. As awful as it was, I took a large gulp. I walked to his table. I was face to face with a legend.

"Good evening, Sir. May I join you?"

"Well good evening to you, Young Sir. Please have a seat." Hornigold's voice was so distinct and his accent; so proper. This was unexpected. He was gentlemanly and not the example of what I had learned of piracy in the last few moments.

"Captain Hornigold, I am honored to meet you. You have no idea how much this means to me."

"You are?"

"But of course, my apologies. I am Eli Ellis. I am here to offer you my services."

"Your services? You do not look one bit like a scalawag. I take it that you are not a pirate. Do you seek to sell me something?"

"No, no Sir. I seek no coin from you. I am here to give you something."

"And that is?"

"Immortality."

"So then, you are a warlock? Pardon me but, I am no follower of spells. I believe them to be silly."

"No, no Sir. I have nothing silly to offer and I know no spells nor have I ever seen any proof of their workings. I offer your name . . . immortality. The name Captain Hornigold will live forever."

"And how would a young boy, no older than 12, offer me such a powerful gift?"

"I'm 15. And I am to be your scribe."

"My scribe? Explain yourself."

"I read and write very well and I am well versed in writing in the ways that those do in pamphlets, gazettes, and even those famous enough to have their own books. I want to sail alongside you. I want to keep a journal of you. I have been reading about your exploits since I was 8. You are my absolute favorite and I am humbled to even be at your table. If you would allow me the chance to do this, you would see . . ."

"Fine. I think it is a splendid idea."

"You do?"

"Yes, you can serve as a cabin boy to me. As we land at each port, you will drop off your writings. You must make three copies of each. One to be delivered to ports and printers, one for you; one will go with me for my personal effects."

"Yes Sir, I will do whatever you ask of me. I am once again honored and it was my belief that it would be much harder to convince you to use my services."

"Well, it might have been the case if you had met me earlier. But I am at a crossroads in my life. There are many changes coming to the business of piracy, privateering, and general trade. I am to evolve with this change if I want to survive. You will be writing the first story of its kind. This I promise."

"What changes will you be making?"

Our conversation was disturbed along with all that were in the room. A large man that stood shoulders above all pounded his fist into the center of a card table and it split in half. No more damage could have come from a cannonball. I had never seen anything like him. I was unsure if his height was of God's making or if the rum and smoke had taken its effect.

His head was near the ceiling. His shoulders were as wide as the door. His beard was black, long and thick. The cutlass on his hip hung to the floor and his chest was burdened with no less than five pistols. This was every man's nightmare.

The monster yelled. "If you ever cheat me again, I will strangle you, skin you alive, and then boil you. Do you hear me?"

Three men backpedaled on the floor like newly discovered crabs. All were looking up and screaming apologies as if they believed his threats. Coins were still spinning on their sides from the fall but each man pushed the currency his way as an offering.

Captain Hornigold looked at me and smiled. "Even I fear the reckoning to be exacted on the world once Teach is in charge."

I turned instantly. "What do you mean? Why would that beast be in charge???"

"I will be retiring soon. The sea holds other adventures for me."

"But . . ."

"But . . . nothing. If you want to go, you will be on deck tomorrow morning at sunrise."

"Yes, Sir."

To The Sea

From my bedroom window, I could see the waterfront. I stared out of it all the time. I will admit to crying as this could possibly be the last time that I ever did so. My mother, father, and brother; I would miss them all. They were good people and we were a good family. But it was a family in which I never fit.

I enjoyed books, reading and writing; I wanted to see the world. I was small and thin; scrawny was a polite word that I heard often. There was no future in Bath that would make me happy. My mind had outgrown my body and my heart had outgrown my mind. I could not help what it was that I craved. I tried to let their hearts rest as easily as possible in my letter.

With quill and paper in hand, I thought long and hard. I needed them to know that I was safe and that I was happy. I did not want them to worry. I wanted there to be no blame or guilt.

Dear Mother & Father,

You both have been so good to me. You have loved me dearly and provided for me well. I never want you to blame each other or yourselves. This is, in fact, a time to be happy. Both of you know that I have always enjoyed my studies. My heart is with books and literature. Others my age are finding love and starting families. I have found my love and my provider.

I have taken employment as a scribe. I will be on the high seas for long periods of time. I will work the logs and journals for privateers. You both secretly know that this subject has been a favorite of mine.

You will hear from me again so please, do not look at this with terminality. It is not. In addition to writing to you from time to time, I am sure we will take port in Bath occasionally. I will look forward to seeing you and telling you of my adventures.

Thankful, Eli Ellis

I hoped it would be enough. Life is to be lived selfishly. Living the way someone else desires will leave you empty. I would be empty no longer.

My bags were packed. I had taken many items from my brother secretly over the last few months. His growth spurts had allowed him to get new clothing. It was not my fault that I had not grown in the same way. His old clothing made good work wear for me. It was embarrassing to get used items from your younger brother. Now, I was glad that there were extras.

I placed on the black cap that I found the night before. Selfishly, I never tried to return it. Truthfully, I was simply too overwhelmed by all that I had seen the night before and it never crossed my mind.

I stood and looked into the mirror. I instantly saw one thing that I wanted to change. While some of the crew had long hair; braided or not, I noticed that many did not. Some were cut close to their heads. There were even several that were bald.

I removed my cap once more and looked at myself. Without hesitation, I reached into my drawer and *removed the scissors. My ponytail fell to the floor but that wasn't enough. I continued to snip away until the floor around my feet disappeared under a blanket of brown. I would be glad of this when the sun beat down upon me in the following weeks.*

I looked around the room for a final sweep. Then I discovered the hardest thing in which I had found to part with. But they were too cumbersome. I could not take them all. I would have to leave many of my books behind. I must choose four or five. No more.

I laid my book belt across the bed and thought hard. This would be no easy choice. My fingertip moved across each spine with care.

I sat the first book across the belt. Paradise Lost by John Milton had to be amongst the choice. It had the ability to captivate me every single time that I chose to open its gait.

Next, I would choose Leviathan by Thomas Hobbes. I was typically not into politics; as I saw it a constant source of bickering amongst the corrupt. This book, however, offered me hours of deep philosophical conversations that I would have with myself.

I debated for a moment and then finally grabbed

it. Shakespeare's *Julius Caesar* would go. I know that in this day and time, Shakespeare was dated and cliche; but I enjoyed it.

The Misanthrope by Moliere. There was never any doubt that this must go. I could chuckle at the irony of society this book has shown me without even reopening it.

One last choice. I thought hard. Don Quixote by Miguel de Cervantes Saavedra. This was imagination at its finest.

Five books were more than enough. I did not want to come across as dependant upon them. Not to mention, I may collect books from all over the world now. The very thought of the offerings at various ports began to stimulate my mind. I had to focus. I folded the belt around the books and slid the buckle into place. Until I knew what my quarters and spacing looked like, there would be nothing more making this trek.

I glanced out the window again. My eyes began to swell once more. It was not only melancholy that found me. I knew that I was an adult now. I knew that I would be in a better place. I was both using my skill and fulfilling a dream. To be writing about piracy and the high seas was nothing less than a blessing.

The sun glared on the glass in front of me. I could see every spot that had gone uncleaned. Still, though, its imperfections were suddenly beautiful to me. I may never do this again.

Wait! The sun was rising! Captain Hornigold told me that I must be on the deck of the ship or I would be left. I ran quietly to my door and turned the knob. The hallway was a treacherous span of squeaks and moans. One by one, I made every step as softly as possible. Sneaking down this corridor in a small, quiet home was the only way that I could ever feel that my frame carried any weight at all. At the moment, I was humongous.

I placed my hand on the doorknob and to my escape. As I began to turn it slowly, my book belt slipped from my shoulder and knocked over a candle. The crash was unsettling.

"Matthew? Is that you???" My mother's voice sounded instantly.

"No mom, it's just me. I'm going down to the water with my leads to do a sketching of the sunrise. I'll be back in a couple hours!"

"Ok, be careful!"

I wasted no more time. The door closed behind me and I increased my gate across the yard. I had nearly a mile to cover and I knew that they would not wait for me. My importance had not yet been understood.

The last look back that I made to our home was only momentarily; my walking never stopped. I constantly peered to my left and to the water. Bath Creek was there and I had not seen the ship yet so this was a good sign. Perhaps there was something that had delayed their departure this morning. I could only hope.

I had moved quickly and was over halfway to the port when I saw someone approaching from the opposite direction. It was a woman. I could see her dress from the distance. I could only hope that it was not someone that would recognize me. I was almost there and nothing would stop me now.

Dammit all! It was Mary Ormond. I hated her so. We were the same age but our lives could not be more different. My brother and I lived humbly with our parents and were generally happy children that did not complain. We tried to be kind and polite to others.

Mary Ormond was a rich brat. Her father had done well for them in what I am sure to be no more than political corruptness. She was gorgeous and curvy beyond her years. All the local boys liked her and most likely the men as well. Being beautiful did not help her personality at all but I remained unimpressed. She was vulgar at times to me and to any she felt of lesser quality.

I dropped my head and continued to walk faster. Our paths would soon cross and I wanted her to have no memory of me. The hat, the fresh hair; hopefully it was enough.

As we came side to side, I looked to the field on the right. I could feel her examining me. New faces were uncommon. She spoke. "Good morning, Sir."

As she was slightly behind me, I returned. "Good morning, ma'am." I had forgotten the distinction in my mouse-like voice. I kept walking; leaving her behind.

"Wait! Stop! You there . . . I said to stop!"

I thought about running but this would just raise more suspicion. Without looking back, I deepened my voice. "Apologies ma'am but I must be on my way. My ship will be leaving at any moment."

I started to walk once more. I was now at a trot and if she were to discover me, she would have to do so in a sweat. I would not be an easy prey.

"I said to stop! Do I know you? "

Under my breath, I would answer. No, you do not know me, wench. You know nothing about me. You know nothing about where I am going. I am off to a place where you are unimportant.

She would continue to yell until she was far from earshot or had given up. I do not know if there was any recognition or that she was simply insulted by the lack of acknowledgment. That was something that she was unaccustomed to.

I could see Captain Hornigold's ship. The breeze was constant and his flag waved to me personally. I was going to make it. I slowed my walk. I did not want to be without breath when I arrived. I needed to seem settled. The crew that I saw last night had no idea that they were looking upon a new mate.

As I made my way up the boarding ramp, I paused to look at the grappling hooks that held the ship in place. I had no idea that they were so large. Those hooks were poetically symbolic to me. They were all that held me in place.

I was nervous as I made my way aboard. My head

rose over the outer edge and I could see the deck. I had never stepped foot on a real ship. I was surprised to find that the crew was missing. There was not a soul in sight.

I wandered around slowly and with great caution. I peered down below and saw pile after pile of humanity. There were men sleeping everywhere. Perhaps the Captain had chosen to make an exception after the wild night before. Perhaps he was allowing them an extra few moments to sleep.

I made my way to the front of the mighty ship. With each step, I took in everything around me. The ropes; they were much larger than my own arm. These are the things that sketches do not properly teach.

The planks were sticky. I could only imagine the dozens or hundreds of coatings that had been mopped upon them. The salt could be brutal. This much, I knew.

I sat up front and looked at what I could see of Bath. It seemed so tiny from where I perched. I had nothing to compare it to. I had once been on a small boat with my father. We went to the mouth of Bath Creek. I could see where it met the Pamlicoe.

More than thirty minutes had passed. There was still no movement from below. I looked at my books. It seems that I may have a few moments to start a chapter. Today, I would begin working on Don Quixote for what must be the tenth time; maybe more.

I enjoyed my book. It was always a great way to pass time. The sun began to warm my head so I placed it beside me. Soon the reality struck me. I was on page 42. No one had yet moved. I had been reading silently for a while now. I was not one to make trouble on my first day but I did have fears. If my mother found my letter too early, my career would die here on the same morning it was meant to start.

* * * * * * * * * *

I began to worry. I was now on page 81. The sun was no longer on the water or even the treeline. It was overhead. It must be at least 10 or 11. My parents have no doubt began to worry. It is my hopes that they would go to the waterside first. If they saw my letter, they would instantly come to the port. This would not be a suitable ending.

As the ships would come and go, I could see them from our home so I knew that from the ship, I would see my home. I could only pray that it was sooner than later. I began to watch the road nervously. If I saw them *approach, I would have to hide quickly.*

Finally, something broke the silence. The large man that they called Teach came staggering from Ferrell's Tavern and slammed the door. It sat on the water's edge so I easily heard it. He was the monster that destroyed a table with a single, angry crash.

He made his way to the ramp. I quickly placed my book back under the belt and tightened it. With revived spirit, I jumped up and went to meet him.

"Who are you?" His shadow covered me. "I am Eli Ellis."

"Why are you on this boat? You running away, laddy?"

"No. I was hired by Captain Hornigold to become his scribe."

"And why beit a pirate would need a scribe?"

"I am going to handle his logbooks, any government documents, and most importantly, document his travels and journey for the generations to come."

"I find this most interesting."

"Do you now? I'm honored to be here, Sir."

"You'll need to be very comfortable with my name. I am Edward Teach. I shall soon be the most feared name on the high seas. You shall bear witness."

"Mr. Teach, not to stray from the current matter but . . . do you know how soon we will be leaving?"

"You in a hurry to leave, laddy?"

"Yes actually, but please do not tell the others. I'm running off from home."

"Your father; did he beat you?'

"No, he is a very kind man. But I have no future here. Writing and literature is my future. I have always wanted to join a crew at sea and share my observations with others. I know such things do not interest you but . . "

"Never make unfounded assumptions of me. I am very interested. In fact, I am very interested in what you can do for me."

"My apologies. I would have never guessed."

"You see a large oaf in front of you, no?"

"No but . . ."

"I am an educated man, laddy."

"Where did you school if I may ask?"

"El mundo es mi escuela."

"Spanish, Sir?"

"Laddy, do you prefer French? Le monde est mon ecole."

"What?" I was very confused and astonished.

He smiled. "The world is my school."

"Yes, Sir. I understand." I smiled with an impressed soul. Then I remembered the world around us. "So, when might we be leaving? I do not want my parents to find me."

Edward smiled and then walked to the front cabin area. I stood and watched. I did not know if he had decided to dismiss my request to offer aid. He stopped at the door and grabbed the handle on the large bell hanging by what I assumed to be the kitchen. His ringing was powerful and unapologetic. It was deafening.

Men clambered from everywhere. As they became visible, he would playfully scold them or even kick their rears. Captain Hornigold came rushing out and questioned Edward as to why he had disturbed the crew's slumber.

"Come forth quickly, Captain! Your scribe is here and he has expressed his readiness to be at sea. He claims to backhand any man that challenges his demand! Come now!"

Hornigold; the others, they all looked at me in anger. Edward Teach laughed. I wished the good lord would have struck me to be a turtle at that very moment. I would have disappeared into my cave to never return. The lord did not hear my command, however.

"I said no such things about anyone!"

A large, muscular man stepped into my chest. He was bald and had olive skin. His dark mustache curled outward on each side of his face. I believed him to be an Arabian. He grabbed my lapel and lifted me with anger.

Edward Teach allowed the joke to run its course

but then came to my aid as others surrounded. "Relax Umar. Place the rat back on its feet. He has said nothing. I was just joshing about."

Umar had not broken his eye contact with me. I tried to look him in the eye but I was much better at glancing to each side. His anger continued. Then, his ruse ended in laughter. I smiled also. Despite his loud roar, I assure you that I was happier. I would live another day.

All but a few men departed. The rest disbanded and quickly went to their posts. Within only moments, the boat began to shift heavily. Grappling hooks were removed and ropes hit the deck. Sails climbed to the heavens and orders were thrown in abundance.

Teach looked to me and then to those left in our circle. Laddy, this bastard that lifted you in fear is Umar. Umar is Persian. As he twisted his mustache, the large Arabian winked at me and smiled. His teeth appeared to have been amongst the whitest on the boat.

"Here, you have Nafu. Nafu was a slave that we'd taken on some time back but when we saw how useful he was, we decided to keep him on." He wore only a pair of tattered shorts. His hair was a mess and he had a bone through his nose. I know this description was very typical but, he did meet every qualification that I could have ever *imagined.*

Teach continued. He pointed to the side where there was a very rough, older man sitting and talking to himself. His hair was that of salt and pepper; most likely never had seen a brush. His teeth were a mess and his face seemed to be coated in tobacco juice. "That man is Leland. Leland is angry all the time, eats raw fish, and no one can understand what he is trying to convey when he speaks. Steer clear of that one until the fighting starts. Then, he's the one to hide behind. He's a savage."

"And her?" I pointed to a lady; perhaps the only on the ship. As I did, she looked up and smiled. It was the woman that I had seen naked in the alley with the man. She walked up with a swagger and a smile.

"I'm Joanna. Save your coin, boy. The seas can be a desperate place and I will care for you in fine fashion. Just ask any of these gents."

I was dumbfounded. As I peered around and looked each of them in the face, I realized that she had most likely been a partner with each.

"Ma'am . . ."

"No, Joanna. My name is Joanna."

"Joanna Ma'am, you are the only lady on the ship? That must be a lot of work."

"Yes, I'm the only lady here unless they are transporting slaves. Then those boys will wait in line to be with a negress. But . . . that too passes and once again, I am the only lass here. Pays well too."

The men all laughed and then Teach pointed to a tall man with a long, blonde ponytail. "That'd be the one we call Robin Hood. Looks a fair bit like him too I would reckon."

"Yes, I am sure he does."

The old man behind me is Padre. We picked him up as a captive in Hispanolia but . . . he liked it here and felt we needed regular access to The Lord so, he stayed on. Being a holy man, he figured he could help."

"Richard here is our Doctor." He was a clean-cut man and one of the few on the ship.

"And finally, I give you Nimrod. I have no idea what his real name is. We saw him hunt down in Brazil and had to have him. He can hunt, trap, or catch pretty much anything." The man in which referred was nearly

as small as I. He would be a Pygmy of some sort I thought.

****

The boat cut through the water at an astounding pace. As we moved down closer to the mouth of The Pamlicoe River, porpoises darted beside us in play. Along the banks, I saw homes; people standing in their yards. I knew that their hearts must be filled with envy.

To our left, several Tuscaroran canoes made their way down the banks. As we passed, they yelled in what seemed to be angry chants. I do suppose we are still fairly unwelcomed here; treaty or not.

My thoughts drifted back to my home. Had they found the letter? If not, were they searching the banks in hopes of finding me? Did they even realize that I was gone?

The wind beat upon my face. I had not even questioned as to where we were headed. It did not matter truly. I was simply glad to be there.

* * * * * * * * *

In my first few days, I had learned a few things about myself and about piracy. First, I realized that I did not like fish nearly as much as they were going to serve me fish. I also had no idea how often pirates ate eggs. We ate eggs with every meal and in every way. We had boiled eggs, pickled eggs, fried eggs, and even some raw. As a special treat, we would have eggs mixed with . . . fish eggs.

I have also come to realize that I suffer from seasickness with a wicked passion. If you would ever care to experience the foulest of happenings; experience seasickness, over and over on nothing but fish, eggs, and fish eggs.

The crew said that I would eventually adjust to the sea if it were meant to be. While hoping that they were right, I wanted to be just where I was regardless of my maladies. I was a pirate.

Edward had given me a large chunk of cheese that he cut from his wedge. I keep it wrapped in cloth except when I am eating it. I love cheese and I am so glad he had it. He loves cheese as well and eats it throughout the day. It has helped greatly with my stomach issues but has left me barren when it comes to relieving myself.

I have spent more time with Edward Teach in the last few days than what I realized that I might initially. I know that I am officially here for Captain Hornigold but, Edward is an interesting man, to say the least.

He was probably almost seven feet tall. I have never seen anyone that tall. His beard was of the most coarse hair I had ever seen. I thought him to be of white blood, but he was extremely dark-skinned. This may have been from sun exposure. He was born in 1680 in England but came here as a teen with his family. He has an older sister that lives only about a day's ride from Bath.

He was also brilliant. He spoke several languages, he could read and write very well. I was always honored when he would ask to read and review my work. His knowledge of the world, mathematics, and many other things were extraordinary. I had grossly misjudged him from my initial impression. With that said, he could be the monster that I had first assumed.

His temper allowed him to randomly become violent with the crew. He smoked hash quite often and would chew coca leaves as if they were tack candies. He was often destructive. Only two nights ago, he was drinking rum mixed with gunpowder. Moments later, he vomited on the deck and set it on fire. His massive frame held many versions of himself. Still, though, he had become the embodiment of what piracy was for me and I loved every second I spent with him. I felt he had really taken me under his wing as well. After only a few nights of sleeping in the pile of humanity down below, he had allowed me to move my belongings into his cabin.

I knew that Captain Hornigold had to notice that I was not keeping accurate loggings of him in the close manner in which we had agreed but he said nothing. We have pirated two different ships in the last week and all of my accounts were through the eyes of Edward. Both ships allowed our power to go unchallenged. We boarded, took what we wanted, and left. I learned that there was an unwritten code. Pirates would always allow the crews of victim ships to live if they did not fight back. The second that anyone saw Edward coming at them, they lost any will to challenge.

Every night just before midnight; sometimes it was just after, Edward would go to the front of our ship. I had allowed it to go unquestioned until he woke me up tonight on his return. I asked him the purpose of his nightly hiatus. He told me that each night, he sat and spoke to The Devil and that tomorrow night, I would be allowed to visit with him.

The Devil Himself

I sat and waited for hours. My father taught me to always be early. This was proof yet again that he had never consorted with the likes of pirates. For all of the jewelry I had seen taken over the last couple weeks, I now knew why not a soul held on to a watch. It had no importance to them.

No matter. I sat and I read. Still, though, the book could not hold my focus. When the most interesting man that you have ever met tells you that you would sit and speak with Lucifer tonight, your mind tends to lean sharply in that direction.

I did not know how yet to take his words. Sit with The Devil? It was not that I was a nonbeliever. I grew up in the church. I believed in heaven and hell. Therefore, I believed in good and evil and I believed in God and Satan. I simply had no idea if we would really sit and speak with Lucifer tonight or if his words were of metaphor. Simply being around Edward was surreal and I had expectations that anything was possible.

So, I would wait. The night was beautiful. There was wind in our sails from my back and there was a steady breeze on my face from our forward movement. The sea was a slick sheet of ice and the moon owned the sky. Whales charming each other in song had become commonplace. Do not confuse that with boredom. I could not convey the opposite anymore strongly.

Many of the men were asleep but still, many more were talking at the back of the ship and down below. They never approached the front of the boat during this time. They knew it belonged to him and probably would occasionally question my own sanity for being on the bow during Edward's rite. They were all nice to me for the most part but kept their distance. I asked Edward about the reason for this once. He explained that due to my scrawny stature, they all assumed I would be dead soon. He did not blink, nor acknowledge that there was humor in his statement. He was serious. They knew that they should not get attached. They had greatly underestimated me. I was like a barnacle in my attachment to this ship.

With time, Edward finally appeared in the distance. Joanna was with him. They made their way over to me and both sat down; she closely beside him.

"Evening, laddy." He spoke with ease.

"Good evening, Eli." She too seemed relaxed.

"Good evening to you both."

No sooner than I finished speaking, he released his belt and slid his trousers to his knees. She placed her head in his lap and began to pleasure him. I had seen him in his entirety.

As if it were not happening, he looked to me. "So laddy, I have called you here for a reason."

"Teach! Do you not wish me to leave???"

"Leave??? Why would I? I called you here. Do you not remember?"

"Yes, I remember with great accuracy but you seem to be occupied at the moment far more than any conversation that I could offer!"

"No, no, she will be done in a moment. I come here to relax. She is simply assisting. Pay it no mind. No, better yet; she will take care of you when I have finished."

"She certainly will not! I will not . . ."

"Laddy, calm down. I care not how large you are. Show yourself with freedom here. I have no doubt she has seen it all. Your size means nothing to me. If you have truly something small enough to warrant hiding, I know I'd like to see it for myself!"

"No, it is nothing to do with size! I was simply raised with more humility than that!"

"Ahhhhhh, humility. I remember humility. In fact . . ."

He paused and his head went back. One hand went forcibly to the back of her head. The other grabbed my own and squeezed. He possibly even gurgled. Could she really do this to him? She sat up after a moment and went to the bow. Joanna leaned over and spat while he adjusted himself.

He yelled at her. "Waste not, want not!"

She turned around and wiped her chin. "I ate well tonight, Teach. There simply was not the room." Then, just like that; she walked off.

"So Laddy, you and I are about to share a very important talk."

"Yes Sir, I have my journal."

"I see this. I knew this before approaching. You always have your journal. I have all mind that you sleep with it."

"I actually do Sir. And on the subject of sleeping and my quartering, I am very thankful you have moved me into the cabins."

"You are not comfortable with the men?"

"Yes Sir, I have no issues there."

"Have they seen your tiny rope yet?"

"Sir! I simply meant that I feel I am closer to where decisions are made and matters of importance. It is very good for my writing."

"It is your lie to tell, I suppose."

He looked at me and laughed.

"The reason you are here is that I have several things to share with you. There are many important things approaching us in the months to come and our world will change greatly. I will speak to that in a moment. But first, we will convene with Him."

"Him?"

"Yes, we will speak with Lucifer."

I looked around. I felt sick to my stomach. Was he here? Was he approaching? If so, he would see me here on a pirate ship. I had just witnessed a man dump his seed in a woman's mouth. I was sure to be placed on the list for Hell.

Edward pulled out a bottle of rum from his jacket. Beside it, he sat a satchel. He started placing a fair amount of gunpowder in the bottle of rum.

"Why do you do such???"

"Silence boy. You know not of what you speak. This is the way. I learned this in Hispaniola." He went back into his bag and produced four coca leaves. "Now open your mouth."

"I am really quite fine and don't . . ."

"Open your mouth!" I did. He slid one on each side of my jaw. "Now just leave it there to sit. Next, he loaded his pipe and then poured several drops of a liquid on the tobacco and lit it.

"What is that, Sir?"

"Yapian. It's from the east. This will guide us to him." He smiled and worked with haste. I had no idea that he had just drenched the tobacco in a powerful, medical opiate. He lit the pipe and puffed away. Then, he handed it to me. I was not to cower or question him anymore. My draw was not as powerful as his own but it was more than enough. I began to cough uncontrollably.

He laughed. "Just give it a moment, Laddy. Just close your eyes and you will see." I did. When my eyes finally were open, the world was a different place. My own hand struggled to catch itself as I waved it through the night air. The moon, she smiled. She was a beautiful goddess. Then, he handed me the rum I drank like a fish until the taste finally caught me. I was once more coughing and gagging but, I was a pirate. "Laddy, I made a pact with the Devil."

"Yes. The Devil. Where is he?"

Edward smiled and pointed to the crow's nest that towered over the ship. In the day, there would be a man there on the lookout. Tonight, Lucifer was there. He *smiled.*

I jerked away and backpedaled on my rear while yelling. It was horrifying. He was real. Less than two weeks of sailing and I had met the most feared object in history.

"Relax Laddy. He is a friend and means us no harm."

"No harm??? He does not mean to place us in Hell???"

"Hell? No. Far from it. Lucifer is a deal maker. I have made a deal with him. If I fulfill my end, he promises to do the same."

"What such deal is this?"

"Captain Hornigold will be retiring in the coming months. Did you know this?"

"He had made a statement to this general effect, yes. I know of no details."

"Ahhhhhh, the details. Neither do I. But he has promised me that when he does, I am to take control of this business."

"Well, that is good news; is it not?"

"Yes, it is very good news. It's also why I possess such a profound interest in you and your values. I aim to be the most famous pirate in history."

"We can do this together, Sir!"

"Yes, we can. But I possess several dilemmas in which I must meet."

"Such as?"

"First, my name."

"What is wrong with the name Teach?"

"There is nothing wrong with it, or at least there should not be. But the truth be known, not all scribes are as talented as you. Since the war ended years ago and I went into the business with the Captain, I have seen my name written with many mistakes. Teach has become T I T C H E. I have seen it as T H A T C H. I have even seen EDUARDO. I am no Spaniard."

"I see."

"So, we must come up with a name for me." I broke for a moment to see if Satan was still there. He was. He continued to smile. "Look at me you bag o bones!"

"Sorry, Sir."

"We must come up with a name that is known around the world and without mistake. Then, we must tell of the exploits; embellish them if you must. It will be needed."

Why would I need to embellish anything? You are a daring pirate and will make an ominous captain; no doubt!"

"Laddy? Have you ever seen me kill a man?"

"Yes, plenty, well . . . no. But I am sure you have."

"No. Never. Not one. It's part of our great agreement." He pointed to Lucifer and shook his head.

"Tell me! Tell me of this agreement!"

"I cannot be killed."

"Well, this is splendid! We will tell your story for years; decades even! They will believe you to be a specter!"

"I cannot be killed as long as I hold up my end of the bargain."

"And this bargain is?"

"I cannot kill. As long as I do not kill, I cannot be killed. If I ever take the life of another, I will die the most painful death any man has known."

"Why would he do this? Satan, I mean?"

"He did it because we are but monkeys to him. We are the entertainment. He charges to make my life a challenge. I can live this life free of the worry of death as long as I do not kill. He aims to make it most challenging. You see, by nature; pirates kill. They have to at times. He takes away my ability to do what I do best. All the while, promises to allow me to do so forever."

"Madness. How do I fit in?"

"Every take; every raid, you must tell that I have killed five, ten, twenty men. Your reports must strike fear in ways that our world has not known. If our victims know I am of grave danger to them, they will not challenge my authority. I charge you with my life. I charge you with seeing that I live forever."

****

No person has ever felt the pain that I have. I stared at the ceiling through the slow rocking motion of the ship. My head ached with furious passion. My shirt was covered in my own vomit. I could barely swallow through the incredible dryness that was my parched mouth.

As I sat up, I released a suffocating dry heave. I had nothing left to offer. I peered out the window a moment and then down at the floor. The realization hit me that there was land to our left. We were about to port! The silence was broken.

"Well, it's Sleeping Beauty!" Edward exclaimed.

"Who?" I questioned?

"Sleeping Beauty . . . a character by Perrault."

"Yes, I know the story but why did you call me that? Did you not also sleep afterward?"

"Sleep? Yes. I slept like a baby. Then I awoke the next day."

"What?"

"You have been in slumber for six days. I thought you were dead." He bellowed in laughter. "I suggest you clean yourself. We'll be porting in an hour."

"Where?"

"La Florida. You will love this place. We are going have five days of festivities here while the crew does a proper careening."

"I slept for a week???"

"Indeed you did. And that was after only an hour or two of relaxing with The Devil and I. I cannot imagine the rest you shall need after the week ahead!"

* * * * * * * * *

I have never seen anything like this. Everyone just once should see the massive undertaking of a ship amidst a proper careening. Our ship was intentionally ran aground on a sandbar and gently placed on her side. The men crawled the hull over and removed barnacles, algae, and woodworms. The sheer amount of things removed *cannot be guessed until seen in person. They would work through the night and then coat the entire side with tar tomorrow morning while the sun was there to add to its tackiness. The rest of the crew would enjoy the port's nightlife. Tomorrow, the careening would take place on the other side while the crews were allowed to switch. As for myself, the captain and all other distinguished staff, we would enjoy all that the port had to offer night after night. I am unsure of how much enjoyment I could tolerate.*

* * * * * * * * * *

There was a group of us totaling five or six. Some of the other crew was already there and the others would be shortly behind. As we neared, I could hear music from drums, unlike anything that I had ever heard. I did not know if these rhythms originated from Afrika, Hispaniola; Brasil perhaps.

As we made it into the clearing in the trees, there was an entire town of small shacks, shed, and other poorly constructed huts. They formed a large circle that would fit no less than fifty ships and in the middle, musicians, dancers, patrons, and vendors offering things of another world. This place could have no equal.

Edward looked back at me. "Laddy, do you have

your trusted journal?" Hornigold smiled playfully.

*"No. Not here. I feared I may lose it. Don't worry;
I will not forget any of this. It is all engraved into me
permanently. This, I promise."*

*"Yes, take it all in. Tonight will be special. It's
your first port. Anything that you see, I will buy you.
There is nothing here out of your grasps."*

"Thank you, Sir."

* * * * * * * * *

*We sat under a large, open cabana. As the
amusements went forth, I wondered where we would sleep
while the ship rests on her side. The food we were having
was unlike anything that I had ever tasted, It appeared to
be a mixture of chopped fruits with shrimp and other
shellfish in it. I do not think that they had been cooked but
I did what the others did; I ate. They would scoop the
mixture up on some sort of fried cracker or pastry and
therefore, needed no utensil. This food was delicious.*

*I drank ale for the first time and I must say, I see
the appeal. It was most tasty and sat more easily than the*

*rum that was commonplace on the ship. I enjoyed my
meal, the music, and the extraordinary mix of people. At
no time before had I ever been anywhere that there were
fewer whites than non. I would easily suppose the ratio to
be at least ten to one; perhaps more. It seemed to bother no
one else and I certainly felt in no danger. I was a pirate.*

*Women moved in and out through the night;
grabbing crew members and leading them away. They
would return later and rejoin the festivities.*

*A tall, slender Afrikan lady danced in my
direction with the movements of a snake. She wore no top
and her breasts moved with the music. I could not help but
notice the size and length of her large, brown nipples. As
she came closer, Edward laughed and point to me. She
danced with them now touching my face. I smiled at each
of the men to my sides.*

*As she was now straddling me despite my reclined
position, she could only want one thing. I obliged if for
nothing more than to satisfy her and the crew around me.
I pulled her nipple into my mouth and began to suck. As I
did, she wrapped her arms around my head in a loving
embrace. As this occurred, the men erupted in cheer as if I
were a soldier returning home. So little it takes to be a
hero.*

She raised her arms over her head and continued to sway as I kissed and sucked. It felt unnatural; yet not. I knew that unnatural was a term that had no place with us. All things enjoyed were to be done.

She closed her eyes and let her head fall back. I truly believed she was enjoying this. She could not have been much older than me. Edward grabbed my hand and placed it between her open thighs. I did all that I knew to make her happy. It was enough. As I continued to kiss, suck, and mead her crotch into a hot storm, Edward leaned over to kiss her other breast. I felt as if we were brothers in arms. Then suddenly, he bit down hard as if he were a shark. She screamed in pain and leaped back. While she wrapped her arms around her breasts to cover herself, she cried as the men laughed hard. Edward's love of pain knew no ends and the amusement the others gained from it was just as stunning.

****

Night after night went on like this. Rum infused sex and fighting paired with substances of unknown origins were used to keep the men up all night and at rest during the day. We slept in hammocks and blankets just off the beach.

On the last night, I noticed that Edward was missing. He was at the gathering; this I knew. He simply was not with us. I leaned in to question Umar on his whereabouts.

"Where has Teach gone? I have to ask how he would miss the last night at the port."

Umar smiled. "He will take a bride tonight.."

"What??? What do you mean? He's going to get married???"

Umar placed his large arm around me. "Yes, our friend will get married. Tonight, we will find a virgin to be his bride. It is a joyous occasion."

"I cannot believe this! He is going to find a bride tonight and marry her? With no other knowledge of her? How can this be? Will she join us on the ship at sea???"

"Relax boy, just relax. You will see tomorrow morning."

No sooner than our chat had ended; he walked up. Holding the hand of a young, very voluptuous maiden, he introduced her. She appeared to be Indian or of some mixed ethnicity.

"Gentlemen, I give you the lovely Rosa Del Ito. Tomorrow, she will become my bride. We will take a home in the town just South of here."

Everyone greeted her with such friendly emotion. I secretly could not be more disappointed. I felt that Edward had just promised me this expansive career at sea. And to throw it away with someone he does not even know! How could this be? How could he love her?

****

For the first time in my brief history on the ship, all of the men were present. The day before, it had been placed upright. Gulls circled overhead and several members of our crew played tunes of European descent.

Edward stood proudly and waited beside Padre. Then, the music became very ceremonial. She made her way from the rear of the boat. She was beautiful. Although it was unlike any wedding dress I had seen, she had an innocent appeal about her that would have swayed any man I suppose. Her curvy legs could be seen through the sun cutting the fabric and her breasts were perfect.

Padre began the brief ceremony. He did not seem

to share the enthusiasm of Edward and the crew. I could only reckon that like myself; he did not want Teach to go away.

After the rite was over, Edward kissed her passionately; almost too much. If she were truly a virgin, it must have been a bit upsetting to be grabbed and fondled in the way he did. She tolerated it as a good wife should, however.

He then reached his large hands into his pockets. The crowd cheered as if they knew what was about to happen. He looked at the objects that he had just removed and counted them with his opposing finger.

"I have pulled six coins here today. Are you ready gentlemen?"

They roared even louder. I was completely confused. Perhaps this was a tradition that was foreign to me. Perhaps it was a tradition among pirates; a tradition of the sea.

One by one, he tossed the coins into the crowd. The fourth one headed right to me. I caught it without thinking. As I did, they all cheered. As he was done, he pointed to the portal in the floor that led to the crews sleeping area. We all went below and waited. I asked more than once as to what was about to occur. Everyone just laughed. We all looked up at Edward.

"Below, my beautiful bride. They have a gift for you."

She smiled awkwardly but with the glow of a new bride. She lifted her dress just a bit and slowly made her way down the steps. Before she could even reach the bottom, the men had violently pulled her down and to the floor. They quickly ripped the dress from her body. She cried and held on to each piece of fabric as if it would protect her somehow. It did not. I sat and just watched as they raped her; over and over again. This was all a ruse. The crew did, in fact, know what was happening. Padre was, in fact, sad, and Edward had no intention of ever leaving piracy. He was simply feeding the sharks. Although I took no part in the act, I too had selfish enjoyment. My writing would continue. My time with him would continue, and at her expense.

All Things Must Change

It was now June of 1717. I am apologetic that I cannot more accurately inform you of the date. On multiple occasions, I have lost days at a time to slumber. Edward said that the cocktails and combinations that we enjoy affect each person differently and that I should be thankful that my side effects are largely just sleep. It has curbed my eating a lot as well. I have gone three or four days without food with no hunger pains or desires.

At least three times or more, Edward has married the virginal love of his life only to feed her to the wolves moments after. I do not understand why he does this; nor how he could. So brilliant, so much potential and yet so much effort thrown into this repeated ruse. A few moments of laughter for him; savage pleasure for a few, and a lifetime of regret, misery, and distrust for the victim. He may be bound from taking lives but he certainly makes up for it in their destruction.

There are many things that Edward chooses to do that I do not condone. I hope my writings explain this.

When I lift the quill, I have many jobs and many roles. Some of my writings must be official; unemotional. Those are the filing or forms and communications with other captains, governors, etc. Then, I must send reports to the gazettes and papers. In these writings, I must instill fear, explain the chaos; even do as he said and embellish. Finally, there is what you read; my own journals. In these, I mostly try to mirror reality. Doing so, I try to reflect my emotions in these without allowing my feelings to contort the facts. I do not wish the bleedover of viewpoints and duties to take from things that actually happened.

* * * * * * * * * *

Today would be one of importance. I have had the pleasures of meeting several well-recognized pirates over the last few months but now, I would be face to face with The Gentleman Pirate, Stede Bonnet.

I sat and listened to Teach, Bonnet, Hornigold, and several others from the respected crews talk business once their initial greetings were over. All of these men seemed to get along well and have a great relationship. Their relationship seemed to be very amicable.

Stede had explained to our heads that he was

dealing with multiple issues within his business. These were deeply personal revelations that he trusted to explain. Stede Bonnet was a man that could stir just as much interest as Edward; just in different ways.

The Gentleman Pirate was just that. He was a former rich, socialite; a powerful aristocrat that like myself, was seduced by the allure of piracy. One day, he had his fill of his well-manicured life. He took his fortune, bought a ship, and abandoned his wife, children, and estate for the seas. He simply walked away.

After hiring a crew, we were well on his way. Bonnet worked with men every single day; all of which knew more about the lifestyle and the business than he. Coupled with his suave and gentlemanly attitude, he did not always command their attention and respect.

As the months grew on, many of their raids were unsuccessful. Often, their tactics and planning were poor. Other times, they would select targets based on poor information and end up with little to no spoils. They were on the edge of revolt and he knew it.

As he sat and told Hornigold and Teach of his problem, Hornigold explained that his time in this business would be soon to come to an end and that he had no direct way to assist in the situation.

Teach cut in. "I have a solution if all parties here are up to the task."

Bonnet leaned in submitting all of his attention to Edward.

"As we know, Captain Hornigold will be stepping away very soon. In this time, I will be taking control of our business."

"Yes, I am aware. Captain, what will you do afterward?"

Edward jumped in once more. "The clever old man will not say." Hornigold smiled and then Teach continued. "So once he has left, I will be in control of this ship. We are also partnering with Ambera and Anne-Catherine. They will be porting here with us shortly to make it official. With the blessing of all, I would ask you to join our crew also. In one day, we will go from a ship to a fleet. You will still command your ship but under our business. We will make decisions as to our whereabouts, trajectory, etc. We will choose our targets while your crew will benefit from our successes financially. You will learn the ways of piracy. No one here loses."

Stede thought for a moment while rubbing his

chin. He uncrossed his legs and then recrossed in the opposite direction and sipped his ale. Then he questioned. "Teach, you are speaking of doubling, tripling, or more the size of the manpower. The need for bounty and resources alike will be huge. How will we feed such a monster?"

"More men, more ships, more guns, and more power. We will hit more targets and also ones of much greater size. I intend to eventually grow into a flotilla."

"But Edward, a ship can only carry so many goods. Will we find targets that can even satisfy such a hunger?"

"We can and we will. And when that isn't enough, we go even larger."

"How do you go larger?"

"Blockades! Sieges! We do not allow the sea to restrain us. We allow it to unleash us!"

"Your ambition knows no bounds. Am I wrong, Teach?"

I smiled and revelled at his brilliance. I knew that with his Satanic Pact, he could not die as long as he did *not take a life. There was no better way to do so with success than to overpower our victims with others that would do the killing in his place. Moreso, most ships would not even challenge him if they suddenly found themselves surrounded by three, four, five or more ships. He was brilliant.*

All parties shook hands. Soon, Anne-Catherine and Ambera McDaniels arrived and joined our meeting. Ambera sat in her partner's lap the entire time. I found it endearing and enticing. The images of women making love to each other was a beautiful thing to me. I had truly become a heathen.

****

For weeks, our flotilla sat at sea. In my opinion, we had been out longer than normal. I found that they usually tried to port every couple of weeks. This allowed for the replenishment of supplies. Anytime longer than that would put us eating mostly bread. Meats would run short quickly.

Today, July 8th, 1717 started pretty normally. I had a biscuit for breakfast and a piece of tack around noon. More than normal, Edward and Hornigold walked the front of the ship together. They seemed to be hunting something.

*From the crow's nest above, a shout rang out.
"Thar she is!!! Sails abust!!!" Has he blew his alert, the
ship that sat on each side followed our lead.*

*Ambera and Anne-Catherine were now operating
with us and I found their expertise exciting. They were
the epitome of efficiency in battle. Their ship, although
smaller, was one of the fastest that I had witnessed.*

*To our right and rear was Hornigold. His ship,
The Revenge was making great time as well. He too had
taken to the front of the ship. We were working as one and
it was beautiful. I went to the bow to join Edward and
Hornigold.*

*Teach pulled out his spyglass. Hornigold already
had his focused tightly. Both men gazed in silence.
Whatever they were focused on what an object of affection.
Finally, I had to ask.*

"What is it that we are after?"

*Hornigold placed his hand on my shoulder. "We
are chasing a behemoth! We are chasing a juggernaut! We
are chasing a leviathan! We are chasing a whale!"*

For once, Hornigold was the excited one and Edward was the one that showed calm and focus. He leaned over to me. "That my young friend is La Concorde de Nantes. That my young friend . . . is mine."

Even without a spyglass, I could see her over the horizon in our approach. It was massive. I could only imagine the amount of booty that could be onboard. It would certainly fill all three of our ships should it be full. This would be exciting.

* * * * * * * * * *

In just over two hours, we had caught up with her. The two other ships pulled up onto her East and we pulled up onto her West side. The grappling hooks were thrown and latched with quickness.

I looked at Edward and asked. "So, this ship seems of more importance than the others. What precious bounties are to be aboard of her?"

He smiled. "It's not the booty that we are after. It's the ship herself. She is no more than a slaving ship but look at her size. This ship is to be mine. Once this is done, I will be in charge and the captain will take the ship in which we stand and sail away forever. This is my birth.

Let's go. Let's tell the world that Edward Teach has arrived!!!"

"No!!!" I stopped him quickly by grabbing his huge hand.

"No??? Why not??? She has submitted. She is mine for the taking. She belongs to Edward Teach now!!!"

"No. She does not. Never use that name again. Board your ship but . . . tell them that they have been taken by the most feared pirate on the seas. Tell them that they have been taken by Blackbeard!!!"

He smiled. He was reborn and I was his creator.

* * * * * * * * *

There was no battle. There was no fighting. The crew would easily give themselves to us. After boarding, we learned that the ship was drowning in desperation and despair. Between the crew and slaves, they had already thrown dozens of bodies over the edge. Sickness had swept through. The Reaper had played his card here well.

We pulled to a scattered group of small islands that sat only four miles to the West. All of the crew and slaves were unloaded. Our doctor closely had a look at each of them. He wanted to be sure that we were not bringing sickness aboard on our new take.

There were over 300 slaves. Many of our crew took the negresses aside and had their way with them. This constant raping that I was exposed to did not sit well with me but I knew that there was nothing that I could say to stop it either.

Upon investigation, we found that there were several members of their staff that would prove useful. They had three doctors in fact. This would be one for each ship in our fleet. Some of the slaves were ready to swear allegiance in return for their freedoms and we were more than willing to oblige. It would take a large crew to operate a flotilla.

Ambera McDaniels walked up to him and bowed. "Congratulations Blackbeard. We have the things that you have requested. I'll be glad to unload them as they have filled our entire cargo area."

"Thank you. Thank you to both of you fine ladies. Blackbeard is very thankful for your friendship."

Stede Bonnet approached next and extended his hand. "Good Sir, congratulations to you! I am proud to serve under Blackbeard!"

The crews worked behind them loading and unloading the ships. From the cargo area of The Ambera & Anne-Catherine ship came cannon after cannon. There were enough guns and munitions to outfit three or four ships. But to these guns, they would all go aboard the new take. It was a fortress and needed to be armed as such.

They worked through the night to make the transition. All the crews, now four plus the slaves brought numbers to more than six hundred. While the work was monumental, we were prepared.

I did so many really incredible interviews. I had not enjoyed my writing in this way in weeks. I sat and talked to Ambera and Anne-Catherine with starry eyes. They were exhilarating personalities. Each of them had their own unique histories and lives. The ways that each came upon piracy was shocking and each could carry their own in an intelligent conversation. It was all that a scribe like myself could desire.

"Hornigold came to our table. If you have not seen the progress on your new ship, she is a masterpiece. Nearly all of the guns have been transferred, nearly all of the goods and supplies are in place, and I have chosen a small crew to help me get back to the mainland. The rest *shall be at your disposal."*

"Sir, I cannot express my gratitude enough. I still pry further to know why you are choosing to walk away from all of this? Blackbeard had a look of seriousness on his face that was rare but this situation had kept him on edge for months.

"This is part of my sitting tonight. I need to address our crew as well as my future. I need to express all my thanks to you and to let you fully know my plans for the future."

"I do wish you would, Captain."

"I also want to address Eli in this. There are parts of this that need to be published and there are parts of this to never be spoken of again. Eli, do you agree?"

"Of course Sir. I am here only to assist yourself and Edwa . . . , Blackbeard. Simply let me know what needs to be done and how to do it."

"By tomorrow evening, all things should be transferred. I will take the smaller of the ships and head back in. Upon landing, I am to take a paid commission."

"A commission Sir?"

"A commission as Pirate Hunter?"

Blackbeard sat awkwardly for a moment. He would look up at both of us for a moment and then look back down. Then his focus fell on me. I knew his anger was serious because he used my real name.

"And you Eli? Are you to join Mr. Pirate Hunter? Will you be chasing Blackbeard all over the high seas? Is this the way you two shall seek your fame???"

I was stunned. I knew nothing about this and now his gaze fell on me. I may have been hired by Hornigold but this was not of my choosing. I stammered but Hornigold quickly stepped in.

"Edward . . ."

"Blackbeard!!!"

"Yes, Blackbeard. Listen, Eli knew nothing of this and is welcome to go with you. I have kept this decision under secrecy for this very reason. I did not want the crews or you for that matter to have any belief that this would affect them poorly."

"*Affect us poorly??? You son of a bitch, you know our haunts! You know our docks and portings! You know our tactics!*"

Anne-Catherine rang in as well. "Captain, Blackbeard is right. I share all of the love and respect for you that one could have but this could devastate our business. We've sat with you; we've spoken of our plans to come. All of this will have to be altered. I must share in the surprise and shock of the others. This will, in fact, harm us dearly."

Hornigold smiled. "No, this will, in fact, make you all the things of legend."

Ambera interjected. "How do you figure on such?"

He continued. "My name will instantly become one of recognition due to the fact that I have lived this life. All eyes shall fall upon me. I will instantly enjoy success because as you said, I do truly know this business to almost an unfair fault."

Blackbeard rumbled. "And this is fortuitous in what manner?"

"It's fortuitous because you will be the one pirate that I can never catch. I swear this to you now. I will not

ever approach you or offer harassment. The seas are filled with too many fish. I will never; I repeat never come after you or any ship in your fleet. I can become rich without breaking this promise."

Blackbeard offered a more inquisitive tone. "So in this situation, we essentially become the greatest game of Cat & Mouse ever known?"

Hornigold smiled. "If you wish, yes. That will be the job of Eli. He will remain with you. All that I ask is that you not harm my own business. Write your stories with close and daring exploits on each side. Keep the readers and governments focused. Have them believe that there is more to read. Have them scrambling to find the next paper, pamphlet or gazette. Your legend will be told based on the quality of your enemy."

Anne-Catherine shook her head in agreement. "I find merit in what you say. I truly do. But how am I to know that you will not betray us?"

"Have I ever broken my word? Ever?

Blackbeard stroked his long beard and smiled. "I can attest that you have not. I accept your decision with ease and respect. I suppose it is only fair that I also offer you wishes for success with irony."

"No, there's no irony. You should truly wish me success. The more piracy companies that I close down, the less competition there is on the seas."

"Yes, I do see the advantages of this." Blackbeard stood up for a moment and paced. All heads turned to watch the towering man in his gate. "When will you depart?"

"I will be leaving; as I said, the moment that all is ready. I will only be taking the bare needs and a small crew. The rest is yours."

Blackbeard smiled. "We do not need most of the crew or slaves that were aboard the La Concorde. I will leave them here on the isle. I did see on the manifests however that there were three doctors on the ship. I do ask once more that I am allowed to take them. We will be a large fleet and the need for more than one will be true."

"This will be fine by me. Now there is another issue of discussion and celebration. What will be the name of your new ship, Blackbeard?"

"You know that I am always the politician. She will be known as The Queen Anne's Revenge!"

I cut in. I had been sketching as we spoke. "Blackbeard, I have been here with paper in hand. I have an idea for a flag. Those friends and foe alike must be instantly aware of you. This will only catapult your name more!"

He looked it over for a moment as he held it close. Once again, he paced as everyone watched. He extended his arms and held it a distance. Then, he pulled it in up close once more. Then he turned it outward and displayed it to the group. "This is our new flag. This is the flag of The Queen Anne's Revenge."

* * * * * * * * *

We had been at sea for over a week. A swell of pride went through me each time I looked upward at the flag I had chosen. A skeleton stood against the black background holding a spear and stabbing a bloody heart. The slaves below had done a perfect job or creating it. No flag on the seas was as instantly recognized. Blackbeard was my creation. I had more ideas that he was going to love. I rushed to find him.

"Blackbeard, I have something to discuss with you that I believe you will enjoy."

"Yes laddy, what is on your mind?"

"As we approach a ship to raid, I need you to find me. I will prepare you for battle in a way that will instill fear upon them. It will offer them something that they have never seen. Not only will I tell of our exploits; they too will rush to shore to speak of the mystic Blackbeard!"

"Tell me more."

"As the ship comes into sight, we will have an hour or more to prepare depending on if they run or not. During this time, I will braid fuses into your hair and beard. Just before you board them, I will light them. You will appear to have smoke rolling from your head!!!"

"Won't this burn my hair?"

"No Sir, not if I dip it in wax first."

"I love this idea. In fact, I find it to be genius. We will soon get to employ this because I have a large task ahead."

"What is it, Sir?"

"We are going to start this new leg in fine fashion. We are going to ensure that my name rings forever. We are going to attack *The Scarborough!*"

"But why would you take such risks??? It's a military ship!!! And it will have no loot to offer!!!"

"There is no risk. I cannot die. Have you forgotten?"

"But there is no loot."

"There is something more valuable. There is the legend of it all. For a pirate to begin his career by attacking the military will only etch my name in stone and ensure that I am never trifled with."

He walked off and toward his cabin. I looked at the large bell that hung on the ship. It said 'IHS Maria, ano 1709.' My expertise was not in this particular area but I believe the ship to have been built in either Spain or Portugal. I hoped she was ready for the things that he would put her through.

I then walked to her edge to further examine. Her wood and planking were massive; the thickest that I knew of on a ship. My estimates said that this ship must be one hundred feet or more. Maybe even one-twenty. Then there were the guns. Ambera had given *The Queen Anne's Revenge* more weaponry than three ships of normal usage.

I counted upward of forty. Was she ready? Yes. I was aboard the most powerful pirate ship on the seas captained by an indestructible giant. The odds were with us. So was Lucifer.

****

In our new cabin, I had much more room. I had affixed a bookshelf in a way that would allow the books to stay in place, even when the ship was beached for careening. It was quite comfortable. I had placed a curtain to cover the doorway between Blackbeard and I. He was out on the bow and most likely would be for a while. He was having his talk. This gave me time for privacy. I would bathe while I had the place to myself. While he could care less who looked upon his body, I did not share this view.

I poured a quart of fresh, clean water into the bowl. The ship with its great size sat almost completely still; it barely rocked at all. The water barely moved. I grabbed the ball of soap from its paper wrapping. I unfolded a cloth and wet it. It had been blistering hot and I needed this.

Next, I rubbed mint gel on my gums and swished the water around in my mouth allowing the flavor to expand throughout. I loved the feeling of fresh breath although I now found myself not doing so for days at times.

I neatly placed my hat on my cot and then removed my clothing after checking the curtain once more to ensure privacy. I stood there bare and rubbed my body with a heavy lather of soap. I was sure to clean myself in every way. Then one by one, I cleaned every limb of the soapy lather that covered it. As I finished, I stood there for a moment to air dry before dressing. Then it happened. The curtain was violently yanked to one side. It was Blackbeard. He could see me naked and I could not cover myself quickly enough. He saw my thin figure; he saw my hips. He saw my thinly haired muff and he saw my small breasts. He saw that I was a woman.

Give And Take

*I stood there as still as an oak. The candle
flickered to my left and allowed for my glistening body to
be examined. At my feet, there were suds on the floor. My
legs were covered in chills from the air drying the water.
My hand covered my most private of parts, but there was
no denying what was there. My ribs were very visible on
each side. My other arm covered the flattest breasts that a
young woman of my age has ever owned. And my face was
pointing to the floor and covered in tears.*

*He was irate and his face was painted with
disgust. He stomped forward and towered over me. He
grabbed each wrist and yanked my hands down by my
side. As I tried to cover once more, he aggressively pushed
my hands back into place. I had nothing but exposure.
Although my mammaries were nearly shapeless, my
nipples were large and erect.*

*I could not make eye contact and the longer he
went before speaking, the more uneasy I became. He
circled my body slowly. On his second pass around, I*

made an attempt to wipe my tears. Once again, my hand was shoved away. Finally, he came to a stop in front of me.

He reached between my legs and grabbed my mound. "What is this???"

I winced but I did not move. He pulled his hand away and took a whiff of his fingertips. Then, he reached forward and pinched my large nipples. "I asked you a question, bitch!!!! What? Is? This???"

I broke down. "I am so sorry!!!"

"You lying little whore!!! Was this his doing???"

"Who, Sir?"

"You play me for a goddamned fool! Hornigold! Did he put you up to this??? Did he know???"

"No Sir, no one knows. I promise. And between us is how I wish it to stay!!!"

"Why are you really here?"

"Sir???"

"I asked you to tell me why you were really here? Answer now you skinny, bony bitch!!! Are you a spy???"

"No Sir. No trickery. I am here for the reason in which I have always said. I am here to document the journeys of a pirate. And now, I am here to make you the most powerful and famous image in the world. No trickery at all!"

"No trickery??? No trickery at all???" Once more, he grabbed my crotch and shook it as he yelled. "What do you call this??? This by its very definition is trickery!!!"

"No, there was no other way!!! If I had come to you wearing a dress and bonnet, you would not have accepted me. Hornigold would have never accepted me. The crew would have never accepted me!!! Tell me that I am wrong!!!"

He released my crotch begrudgingly and stared up at the ceiling once more, and then back at me. I reached over to grab fresh clothing but he froze me where I stood.

"Stop! I have not given you permission to move, you lying wench!!! You have no permissions to do anything on this ship. I allowed Eli on this ship, not you!!! Yes . . . Eli. This too was a lie. So . . . Eli, what is your real name?"

"I am who I say. I am Eli. My name is Elizabeth; Elizabeth Ellis. My studies and my love are in writing and in literature and piracy has always been a favorite of mine. I am here to serve in the exact ways I have exclaimed."

"What madman would even allow a girl to read and write? This is only an example of what happens when it is allowed. You absolutely disgust me." His voice dropped in volume but his anger continued to swell.

He grabbed me by the wrist and began to pull my little naked body through the cabin and toward the stairs. "I will give you to the men."

I shrieked but then quickly realized that I did not want them to hear such. "No!!! No Sir, please don't. You are Blackbeard and I am Eli Ellis. You are going to do extraordinary things and I am going to tell the world. They will be reading about you three hundred years from now; five hundred; a thousand!"

He released me and I fell to the floor. I sat there on my bottom looking up at him and he, at me.

"Sir, I don't want to be raped. I don't want the men to know anything. I just want to do my part here and

for things to remain as they are. This is all that is required for your life to become everything we have planned. Over the last few months, I have truly grown affectionate of you. If you must have your way with me, then do so. I will gladly submit. But not them. Please."

He laughed through his anger. "Me??? You think that I would fuck you? You absolutely disgust me. You are no woman. Women have hips and they have thighs. They have breasts and they have curves. You are nothing that I could ever lay with."

I erupted into tears. "Edward!!! Your words tear me apart."

"My name is Blackbeard. Do not ever call me that name again. Tomorrow, we will awake and things will be what they were. But just know, I will never trust you again."

"Blackbeard, did you not hear my words? I have affections for you."

"And did you not find my words to be clear? You are ugly and you are untrusted. Now that I know you have such affections, you will be made aware of each and every time that I fuck another."

I began to cry once more.

"Get dressed, Eli! Get dressed now and stop crying like a girl or I swear to God, I will toss you over the edge."

He stood for a moment as I threw my clothes on and then he turned to me before leaving. "He was right about you."

"Who??? Who else knows??? Please tell me!"

"Lucifer. Lucifer knows. He sent me here to find you. He will punish you for your treachery."

"How? How will he punish me?"

"One day, you will receive a bargain of trades just as I did. You will be given a choice."

"Why would he do this?"

"He will do so because I am going to ask it of him."

"Please tell me how to fix this. I need to make it right. I need for you to trust me."

"I gave you trust. Now . . . I know not what to

even call you."

"You call me Eli, Sir; Eli Ellis. That is still my name. That is who I am."

"Running around; pretending to be a man. You ask yet still to be treated as a man. Is that what you want? Is this really what you want? You have seen how I treat men that I become angered with, have you not? I beat the shite out of them! And with you, there'd be nothing left if there were no shite."

"Sir, I still beg you to rethink me. I had no other way to convince Hornigold to bring me on. I had to be a man. As a woman, he would not have considered me. And even if so, I would have been no more than a sexual morsel to the men. This way, I am safe to do my job. I am safe to make Blackbeard the most recognized man alive."

****

I awoke like I did any other morning and went through all of my normal routines. I heard him on the other side of the curtain doing the same. I had declared that I would not be the first to speak. There was no need. All had been said and yet nothing had been accomplished.

He hated me. He felt betrayed. Still yet, I would find a way to make myself of value to him.

I knew today would be the day that we would make contact with one of the most ominous ships any pirate would ever approach. By all calculations, we would have the HMS Scarborough within our sites before we knew it. We had believed to have seen her yestereve but, it was far too dark to pursue or attack. We had held our course and knew where she was headed already. So it was time she finally met her match.

What we were doing was insane. The Scarborough was built at the Sheerness Dockyards. Their unbreakable hulls are that of legend. It had at least 30 guns. The Royal Navy's finest, Captain Tobias Hume was leading the way for her. Records show that it was a fairly new ship being built in only 1711 and she had no weaknesses to be seen.

We were not without the ability to hold our own. The Queen Anne's Revenge was gigantic. Her hull had to be just as thick. We were now sporting over 40 guns if you should count some of those lighter in poundage. And we had one more advantage, we had Blackbeard.

While I probably did not do enough to promote it, there were also two more distinct advantages to be offered. We had The Revenge to our left captained by Stede Bonnet and we had The Tree Of Woe to our right captained by Ambera and Anne-Catherine.

The signal was given from the crow's nest above. There was a positive spotting. The two ships sitting in our rear flanks were told to fall in line behind us. We wanted to approach as hard and fast as possible without The Scarborough having recognized that there were two more ships at our tail.

Only twenty minutes had passed and The Scarborough had chosen to not flee. There she was sitting broadside; she dared us to attack. This would not be of issue. He was foaming at the mouth.

Blackbeard saw their positioning and knew that they had chosen to do so for good reason. This would allow them to fire all guns from that side at once. Through our spyglasses, we could see that they were further prepping by moving guns from the other side to face us.

The choice to heavily arm, even over protect only one side of their ship was just what we wanted. Blackbeard gave the command and sent The Revenge and The Tree of Woe in different directions. The Revenge and Bonnet would move toward the front of their ship and begin to fire. The fastest of our fleet, Ambera and Anne-Catherine would circle to their weak side to prepare for boarding. We would meet them head on and absorb the fire like the titans we were.

I will tell no lies. I was frightened. This was not the first take or boarding that I had seen but with all truths told, most ships did not resist. We were now challenging the might of The Royal Navy.

They fired and it tore through the sky. The accuracy they presented was uncanny. With a rough count of at least ten guns firing, two blew through our upper sails on the first attempt. The men scrambled to make adjustments with the roping; much of what I will admit to not understanding.

Blackbeard yelled at me violently. "Well boy, don't just stand there. Grab a sabre or musket. We'll be on her in just moments!" Although I did not like being addressed in such a shrewd manner, it was pleasing in more than one way. First, I understood that this was the heat of battle and he would have spoken to anyone in that nature at the time. Secondly, he addressed me as 'boy' and I could not be happier. Perhaps he had let it go. Either way, he would be keeping my secret.

Several of us scrambled to the front of the ship and behind the ledge. I watched the others ready their firearms and tried to do the same. I had only shot a weapon once or twice in my life and then, it was only after my father's careful prepping.

The Royal Navy fired first. With the crack of many explosions, a plume went up and our deck and hull were rained upon like hail falling in a July storm back home. Then, in tandem, we all raised our guns quickly over the ledge and did the same. I could not tell you if I had actually hit anyone or if any of us did. I do know that they were successful regrettably. As I scoured by down, I realized that I was sitting beside a man missing most of his head.

They returned fire quickly and the wooden wall that protected me splintered at my face. Still, though, I was safe. When we returned to the surface to meet their challenge, we could see the look of shock on their face and it was two-fold. First, The Tree of Woe & The Revenge had fully taken them by surprise and we are now almost in position. It had happened too quickly for them to adjust. Secondly, Blackbeard was standing on a platform up front with his trousers down and showing them his arse. He had no fear.

We were now only fifty feet from them and had begun to take a broadside position as well. Ambera and Anne-Catherine's crew were tossing grappling hooks onto their ship and The Revenge was unloading six, eight, and even twelve pounders relentlessly.

For the first time in history, she came alive with the call of Blackbeard's shattering voice. The Queen Anne's Revenge unleashed hell upon the hull of The Scarborough. Splinters blistered everywhere and their entire ship tipped backward. We were careful to not aim across the deck and bow because The Tree Of Woe was preparing to board across from us.

We fired again and the target rocked violently in the water. The fear on the faces of their men could now be seen. One could only imagine the surprise of becoming prey after always being the hunter. They were in foreign waters, to say the least.

Another man standing beside me was hit with what appeared to be a two-pounder. He exploded instantly and showered me with his blood. I quickly ran to grab his place at the cannon that he had manned. The ballshot was so heavy but I managed to pack and load it quickly. As I lit it, I did not realize that the recoil would be what it was. As it fired, the heavy mule slid back in its drop slots and sent me flying backward. I flew more than ten feet. I needed Blackbeard to see that they needed me as much as any other man on the crew.

Suddenly, The Scarborough tilted to our side and

leaned over to make contact with our ship. Our crew began to toss grappling hooks as well but Ambera McDaniels would not be bested. We could now see her crew from across the length. Using some sort of catapult, she actually had her men fire her onto the deck of The Scarborough! I have never seen anything like that! From a distance of at least 25 or 30 feet, her small frame hurled through the air with her sabre swinging and slashing ahead of her. She hit the deck rolling and came up violently.

Her distraction was executed perfectly. As all eyes fell on her, Anne-Catherine and the rest of the crew boarded with ease. Upon the site of her suicide flight, Blackbeard laughed loudly and yelled to his own. "Look men and look hard at this fiery bitch; for she has bested you all! Attack with grit and perhaps you too will live in the legend that she has created here today!!!"

He did not like to be bested but he also respected these two ladies more than anything. Anne-Catherine had already killed three or more men. Her long, dark hair would sway each time she swung her sword and it seemed to energize her men without a word spoken.

Tobias gave orders and suddenly, soldiers flooded from the decks. He was much more heavily staffed than we had suspected. We were now truly involved in a fight. The hulls of The Scarborough and The Queen Anne's Revenge collided and our men were now pouring across as well. No sooner than we began to climb across, Stede Bonnet and the crew of The Revenge were doing the same. His small sloop had locked itself in place and the soldiers were being surrounded from three directions.

Tobias yelled to Blackbeard from one mass to the other. "What sense does this make??? We have no bounty!! We have no booty! Where will you find glory or good in this???"

Blackbeard returned. "You have something far more valuable!"

"Please divulge this to me! For I am lost as to how you see any gain here!"

"You hold my legend! You are The Royal Navy! Your loss holds my namesake!"

"You are insane!!!" Tobias knew that there was no longer any words to trade with Blackbeard. This was not a conflict that would be reasoned. He looked down to his soldiers. "Kill them all!!!"

Our crews were now on their deck everywhere and theirs were on ours. The clashes were violent to place things lightly. This was the first time that I had seen so much blood. Umar and Leland fought like savages. It began to almost seem as a stroke of luck to see a man die quickly. Many more moved sluggishly to defend themselves through their own injuries. Stabbings, gunshots; nothing stopped them. This would be a fight to the death. Then, everything went black for me.

* * * * * * * * *

I sat there and fell in and out of consciousness. My hands were bound behind my back. I lifted my head once more and could see others being held captive as well. The fighting had stopped. There were no more cannons, no more guns, no more yelling and no more clanging of the sabre. We were now at rest, but at what cost?

"Where are we?" Umar leaned into the man beside him. The man shook his head with a negative response. Suddenly, Robin Hood made a "Shhhhhh" sound to quiet us. We could hear men talking. I recognized Blackbeard as one.

"This isn't our ship. We're aboard The Scarborough. Look at the storage barrels. Those are from England. We've been taken hostage." I emptied my soul

and gave them a dose of the truth.

Umar spoke up once more. "Then we will soon be hanged. Blackbeard does not negotiate. I have seen this twice before. If you find yourself captured, he will not ask for leniency. We are nothing to him. Three ships, three crews; he has plenty of manpower without us. There is nothing to barter here."

I added a positive note; the only one I had. "This may sound true but listen, they are talking. Perhaps he has found value in us."

"Are you truly insane? Are you mad? He will in no way have us back aboard. There is no bounty here, there is nothing to trade. We do not even know if the battle was won or lost." Umar seemed frustrated with me.

Then, black boots came down the stairs. It was Captain Tobias. He had two other soldiers with him. After those came Blackbeard. They all looked upon us for a moment.

Tobias pointed at the men, one by one and as he did, they were cut loose. As they became free, Blackbeard pointed to the steps and up they went. Eventually, I found myself there alone.

"Go ahead, free my cabin boy as well."

Tobias smiled at Blackbeard with a sinister gaze. "Your cabin boy?' Do not try to be coy with me. This is no cabin boy."

I was petrified. How did they know? Blackbeard seemed just as confused. He questioned. "What is it that you mean? He is my property, my cabin boy and I require him back just as you released the others. What is your fascination here?"

"My fascination is that your cabin boy is not what you say. In fact, he is no cabin boy at all. We found a journal on him."

"Your point?"

"My point, Dear Blackbeard is that he is your scribe, isn't he? We have logs of your whereabouts and doings for months. No, this is far more than a cabin boy."

"What is it that you want. You have given me back the rest of my crew and I have returned yours. Now you are the one in violation here."

"No, not quite. We will return the boy but we will keep the log. The log was no part of our negotiations so as

I see it; it is ours to keep or to barter another deal with?"

"Speak your mind, Tobias. What do you want?"

"We will return the journal and in return . . .
today never happened."

"What do you mean?"

Tobias stroked his chin. "I am not prepared to tell
my superiors that I have been bested by pirates. It is my
duty and charge to protect the seas. What would anyone
think if it were known that The British Navy could offer
no assistance in such matters."

"I will tell you what will happen. The Legend of
Blackbeard will grow! My business will grow!"

Tobias smiled. "This is the site of your error. It
actually won't help you at all. If The British Navy cannot
offer some sort of protection, insurers will fear these seas.
They will push businesses for rerouting. Soon, you'll be
sitting here in the sea all alone."

"You utter words of fear. We have bested you
today. How will you explain your damages?"

"The damages to The Scarborough are something

that I can handle. I will return your journal and your scribe. But if I do indeed hear a word of my defeat, I will publish all that we have learned from your precious cabin boy and his writings."

"Then what keeps me from killing you right now?"

Tobias laughed once more. "Your men have already been sent back to your ship. Who will kill me? You cannot?"

"You are foolish enough to believe that Blackbeard, the most feared pirate on the sea would not easily slash your throat???"

"No, you cannot. You are not allowed. You have your precious little pact with Satan." He laughed loudly. Blackbeard boiled.

Before I realized what had happened, he backhanded me and split my lip.

"Why Sir??? No!"

"You are an embarrassment to me. Grab your journal and go!" I quickly scurried up the stairs and he came behind me. We approached the ramp to crossover. He grabbed my shoulder and spun me around to face him.

"If you ever fail me again, I'll kill you."

A Lo Hecho, Pecho

I knew his words were spoken in anger and that in his eyes, I had costed him plenty of bragging rights. But at the time of his negotiations, he knew nothing of the journal. He only knew that I was missing. There was a small part of me that wanted to believe that this is why he even entertained a prisoner swap. Umar even admitted that it was something that he had never done or even considered. I could only hope that he had feelings for me. I do know that mine continued to grow for him.

Upon boarding The Queen Anne's Revenge, I came straight to my cabin and went to sleep. I heard him rummaging through things a couple times during the night but I laid there in silence. More than once, I wondered what to be the thoughts of the men. We were all captured but they were released without incident. I, on the other hand, was held behind. The ship may be big but it's still a very small world asea and the men had to notice.

He had arisen even earlier than normal the morning after. Even from my cabin, I could hear the sails whipping in the wind. They were the strongest that I had ever heard. The sun was glaring in through the door and the water was choppy. I could hear it lapping against the hull of our ship despite its thick construction.

Like every morning before, I quickly dressed and went above. The men were cleaning and repairing from the battle before. How ominous it is to watch and man on his hands and knees with soap and water, removing blood stains from the deck. It was thoughts like this that could get stuck in my head. Yesterday, you were alive and amongst those that you laughed with, worked with, and drank with. Today, that shipmate is working feverishly to remove the last piece of your existence. Wrapped in linens, you were resting on the sea's floor. Perhaps you saved the life of the man erasing you. Perhaps you saved my own.

Sails were being mended, lowered and hoisted, block & tackle were clanging, and other equipment from above being moved and shifted from one position to another.

As I walked around atop the deck, the men made little eye contact with me. Those that looked up would quickly go back to what they were doing; almost intentionally. The prisoner exchange had definitely been of some discussion and I apparently now had the appearance of being more important than the rest. This was the last thing that I wanted. Our ship; any ship needs unity. Still, though, they had to appreciate the fact that we were now all back together and everyone was accounted for versus being left to hang. This had to be a happy consequence that they could see.

* * * * * * * * * *

August 14th, 1717. Today, I realized that I have never been at sea this long or have gone such lengths without seeing land. We have had seven takes since The Scarborough incident and all were very bountiful. We have barely seen a ship in the last two weeks.

He had not spoken to me in any way that was not of direct need. He would give me orders, I would ask for directives; that was it. I tried to accurately document our happenings and I believe I did so as best possible. Today, I needed to make things as they were. I had decided to seek his ear. He agreed to meet with me but was not specific as to when.

* * * * * * * * * *

He sat there at the front of our ship staring into the moon. The air was fragrant with all of the aromas that

I knew he used at this time each night. He did not see me. I watched from a distance. He began to commune with The Dark Angel. Not having used the mystical cocktail, I saw nothing. Still, though, this did not make me believe it anymore or any less. I allowed him to have his rite.

On and on, he babbled. He would look at at the mast and argue. More than once, he shook his fist into the air. Other times, he was barely audible. I knew that he was influenced by the things that he had put into his body and I knew that I too was under such an influence that night. But there was something so real about it. This is why I have chosen to not pass judgments either way. He did not stumble across this technique. He learned it from a master of dark arts on one of his voyages. There had to be more to it than pure trickery of the mind. Not all would have the same revelations.

Finally, he seemed to be at rest. Still sitting and propped back on his arms, he appeared to be barely alive. I did not worry. I had seen it too many times. Now was the time to approach him and end this uncomfortable situation.

"Hey there, old man. It surely is a beautiful night." I toyed with him. He looked up but barely grumbled. I went and sat beside him in the same place I did on the first night.

"I need things to be normal between us. I want them the way they were. I have done everything that I told you I would. My gender stays hidden and has in no way impacted my performance here. In battle or siege, I even try to hold my own there as well. It is not good for either of us to walk around in avoidance of each other. I will best do my job the more closely I am to you. If you want the world to know you, I must know you."

"I know laddy, I know. I'm just hurt. Or at least, I was."

"So then, you are not hurt anymore? I have truly been forgiven?" The excitement bled from my every pore.

"Relax now, laddy. You are still nothing but a cunt to me . . . but you are a cunt of value."

"Yes, Sir. I must ask, you seem to hold the utmost respect for Ambera, Anne-Catherine, as well as other lady pirates. Why is it that I must remain a secret?"

"Those have all established themselves before me; without me. Not to mention, they are not allowed to be active parts of our raids on The Queen Anne's Revenge."

"Why?"

"The men. Many still feel that women are bad luck. If you come to reveal the truth to them now, they'll all feel I have deceived them. They will think of me as your lover."

"Is being my lover so bad?"

"You are ugly."

My head sank down toward my lap. His words were devastating. I thought he was perfect. He was everything a man should be. He was tall, dark, full-bearded, wide-shouldered, intelligent and worldly. Apparently, I was nothing. Less than even.

"How could you say that to me?" I placed my hand on his.

"Do not torture yourself, laddy. I like women. Even undressed, you are a mere boy. I need firm hips and large breasts. You have nothing for me."

"I have seen how you treat women. This is because you do not love them. I could love you; the real you. I could make you happy."

He took a huge swig of rum. "Doing as I ask will

make me happy; nothing more."

"You make me so angry. It is as if you have me frozen in time. I am only what you first saw me as. You won't allow more of me."

"He barked. "That is of your choosing, not mine. You began with this lie and now you will have to live it."

"This will not always be my appearance. I will have all of those things you wish one day. In fact, I became a woman two months ago. I am now visited by Mother Nature monthly."

"The sharks will be happy, no doubt."

"Ugh!!! You frustrate me so! "

"I am protecting myself here."

"You only think of yourself always! How are you protecting yourself to not allow me to be the woman I am?"

"Lucifer has shown me my own demise. It is at the hand of a lady. I feel I am doing my part to keep it at bay if I have covered the fact that you are less than a man."

"Less than a man??? You truly do think nothing of me!"

"I think of you what you have given me to think. You are a lie; a ruse. You are given the respect that you have earned."

"And if I tell the other men?"

"Then I will act as surprised as they and I will have them toss you overboard. I told you before, If you disappoint me again, I will kill you; even if it does not come at my own hand."

"I just do not understand how you could say such things and feel such hate in the direction of someone that thinks so much of you."

"If you think so much of me, you will not betray me."

"I will never betray you; this I promise. I love you."

"And for this, you are stupid."

"Edward!"

"It's Blackbeard."

"Yes, it is Blackbeard. I if anyone should know it."

"Yes, I am the great Blackbeard . . . you're creation, no doubt. But you cannot love me. I do not seek to be loved. If you love me, then I have not shown you who I truly am."

"Oh, I see you. I know who you are. This haunts me daily." I must admit to being quite pitiful at the moment.

"I have a new task for you, laddy. One you will enjoy."

"What is this? Anything! Tell me."

"Well as you know, Padre was lost in The Battle Of Scarborough. We need a replacement. You have a Christian upbringing."

"So then, I shall chaplain the men when they need to talk? When they need ministering?"

"No."

"Then what?"

"You will facilitate all of my weddings from here on."

"How cruel could you be to me??? Are you mad? I tell you how I feel about you and then you choose to include me in your lies and trickery? You are essentially asking me to rape these women!"

"Yes, and you will do it."

"You have some nerve!"

"Perhaps this will soften the way you feel."

"I beg of you, do not require this of me!"

"It is done. It is now part of your duties."

"I'll never forgive you for this!!!"

"You will. I have forgiven your ways. Now, you will forgive my own. We are off the coast of French waters and will soon be in Mexico. Remember one thing...."

"Sir?" I asked begrudgingly.

He smiled. "A lo hecho, pecho."

****

September 22, 1717. We had spent quite a bit of time off of the coast of French Louisiana; much longer than expected. The reapings in this area were so easy and so bountiful that we could not resist. Time after time, his flag was seen and they would simply surrender. There had been no shot fired in weeks. We approach, board, unload, and move on.

I for one was happy about the takings, but even longer that we had been asea for an extended period. This kept me yet from even once performing my pastoral duties. The thought of it made me hate him. Any time that it was not in my thoughts, I loved him.

Now, the word was out. Ships tried to avoid the area altogether. Our welcome was worn and our presence known. The Northern Gulf Area was no longer profitable and we would be forced to move on.

I would miss the food though. Back home, I had eaten crawfish many times. Here, it was different. They were huge and mixed with spices and peppers. Every evening, our men would take small boats ashore and return with an abundance of delicious bounties. We had overharvested the seasides with our piracy so intensely that we found it far too risky to send the crew to the banks as a whole. Blackbeard had become the face of horror in the area. Tonight, the anchors were lifted and the winds would take us all to a new and exciting land.

****

October 2nd, 1717. We could see the shores of Mexico and it was a very welcomed site. Although piracy was in no way anything new to this new world, the word of Blackbeard had not yet been exploited there yet in the same way as to the north and east. Perhaps this was largely due to a language barrier as well as many other things. There, our sails were as welcomed as any other.

Upon leaving the French sector only a week or two earlier, the boat crew had brought aboard two cats and they were now brave sentinels that worked the ship for rats and mice. They did so in fine fashion.

On the edge of sunset, we could see lanterns and torches burning, the beach was littered with huts, cabins, docks, and boats. Wherever we were was well populated and most likely the exact ingredients that our crew was seeking. I could see at least a day or two, but most likely more festivities. While this seemed great and was part of the reason many chose this life, I know that it could finally lead to me being forced now to execute my new matrimonial duties.

****

November 17th, 1717 was our last night there. This has been a very odd time in my life. I have tried to distance myself from him. My affections have grown too strong and therefore I found myself steered by them more than my duties to Blackbeard and the crew. I would torment myself night and night for someone that had openly told me that I would never mean anything to him.

While still upholding my duties in updating the logs, I did not apply my pen to his personal accounts and ways nearly as much. To further that, he had been ashore for over a month with no piratical activities. I was beginning to wonder if other ship; other pirates and their crews would typically take such long hiatus.

I was beginning to understand one of his major problems. While this may purely sound like an excuse, I have grown to learn that the repeated usage of opiates can actually take a hold on you. This may sound like petty excuses to those that have never used, but it can truly take a devil's hold on the mind. It served as an excellent way to keep your mind off of things and I found myself wanting to inhale it's sweet smoke more and more. In what seemed so long ago now, he had taught me how to use it with tobacco and I would drift away for hours.

We all had so much coinage at our disposal and everything was so available there cheaply. I knew that I had formed an addiction to this horrible substance but I saw no way to remove myself from it. Couple that with the fact that I worked for and pined for a tyrannical madman that would also force it upon me if he had any leanings that I was trying to free myself from its chains.

Now, he had announced that it would be our last night on these beautiful shores. I knew that tonight, he would magically fall in love. Tomorrow morning, he would make her the happiest woman alive and then send her ashore as a battered woman; raped and beaten. One that would spend the rest of her life fearful to love again. What insanity was I cursed with to love such a man?

****

I watched him at his cabana. He had already been absent for more than two hours and I knew that he was on the hunt. I was correct. A couple of hours before midnight, he returned with his prize. The unfortunate chosen one *was very short, curvier than most, and most likely even younger than I or at least donned the appearance of.*

He disgusted me. She sat on his lap and I could see that she was showing everyone her new ring; stolen loot no less. She stood up and danced with him to the lively music that bounced across the sand. He would twirl her like a child's toy and her smile only grew. One by one, members of the crew came over to cut in and share in her excitement. Little did she know that soon, many of them would share her in so many different ways. And through it all, I still wished that I could be in her place; at least for the dance and to own his attention.

* * * * * * * * * *

I stood there on the bow overlooking the short strip of water between our ship and the beach. Umar and Leland were rowing a small boat with her aboard and they had nearly reached The Queen Anne's Revenge. The sun was the second brightest thing in the air; only behind her smile and jubilation. I held my Bible awaiting to destroy her.

They escorted her aboard as she made dainty steps over the ledge; politely lifting her dress. It was long and flowing, all white. Her hair was pulled back tightly and decorated with flowers from the land. It was the last moments of her happiness that she would remember for ages.

They led her to a small cabin where he waited for the music to start. First came the violin and then two lutes. They were playing O Rosa Bella. How fitting. Blackbeard came out first in all black attire. He was looking thinner which only added to his height. I believe that his lifestyle was slowly catching him. He walked to me and took position. He looked at me with the most evil of smiles. This man knew what he was doing to me. I would never stop paying the debt for my trickery and lovely maidens from around the world would never stop paying their debt for the crime of simply being female. He hated us all.

Blackbeard whispered to me. "Good morning, Padre. It's a beautiful morning for a wedding, is it not?"

I ignored him and looked away. He continued to rib at me.

"Did you see her? She's perfect. So much a woman, she is. Her curves, her hips, her breasts. Her parents know not that she is even here."

"What???"

"Yes, I met her at the market before sunset yesterday while buying supplies. I told her that I had instantly fallen for her. Within an hour, she had bought a dress. She left her house early this morning before sunrise . . . just as you did. All this just to be with me."

My blood began to boil. I wanted to tell her but I knew that it would be my every demise. If so done, he may have me killed. Even if not, I would be punished harshly or even cast away.

As she walked toward her fate in oblivious elation, his words slapped me over and over. She was stunning. Her hair, perfect. Her neckline and bare shoulders, perfect. Her dress was heavenly and her curves were just as he had stated. She was barefoot and had anklets on each leg. I had no doubt that those would be taken during her rape and possibly reused.

"Dearly beloved, we have come together in the presence of God to witness and bless the joining together of this man and this woman in Holy Matrimony. The bond and covenant of marriage was established by God in creation, and our Lord Jesus Christ adorned this manner of life by His presence and first miracle at the wedding in Cana of Galilee. It signifies to us the mystery of the union between Christ and His Church, and Holy Scripture

commends it to be honored among all people.
The union of husband and wife is intended by God for
their mutual joy; for the help and comfort given each other
in prosperity and adversity; and, when it is God's will, for
the procreation of children and their nurture in the
knowledge and love of the Lord. Therefore marriage is not
to be entered into unadvisedly or lightly, but reverently,
deliberately, and in accordance with the purposes for
which it was instituted by God."

"I charge you both, here in the presence of God and
the witness of this company, that if either of you know any
reason why you may not be married lawfully and in
accordance with God's Word, do now confess it."

The crew went wild and cheered. They knew that
they would soon get their gift. Prematurely, they hooted
and threw their hats into the air. The lovely bride had
never been more radiant.

Blackbeard bellowed and when his laughter came
to rest, he spoke. "Let this be over, Padre. I am ready to
give my new bride her gift!"

"Then let it be. You are now man and wife."

He turned to his bride and kissed her deeply. "So
my love, I have a gift for you. Please, choose any number

between one and ten."

She smiled. "Seven."

He reached into his pocket and removed a handful of coinage. He counted out seven pieces and the rest were returned. One by one, they were tossed into the savage mob. Then he addressed the group.

"You seven men, go now down below and prepare the gift for my bride!" They yelled and screamed. As they went below, he took her by the hand and led her into the doorway. He kissed her once more with passion. Then, he violently shoved her down the stairs. Her screams began and I shuttered.

"The rest of you, chum the waters."

I turned to him quickly. "Chum the waters? Why?"

"When they are done, she will be fed to the sharks."

"Why??? Why would you do this? You are nothing but a coward!"

Before I could finish my sentence, he had

backhanded me with the force of a mule. As I lay, I could see the crew staring at me. I quickly stood up.

"I am so sorry, Sir. My apologies."

I knew that I had to make peace with him and do so instantly. He was getting worse. The madness in him was growing. I need not be a target of his. When we arrived here, he was not well in his head. Now, I knew that Mexico had killed a part of him. He was losing weight, his eyes were hollow. He had lost his soul and would do anything. I would not find myself on the cross side of him again.

The Lost Time

February 11th, 1718. I will start out by apologizing to any who read this logging. We have been in Brazil for months now. His nightlife has taken on a whole new level. Upon leaving Mexico, we had nine very successful takings and it has allowed the men to live here like kings without consequence.

I have taken refuge in a local inn and not heard from him for some time. I glance out the window several times a day to make sure our ship still rests there. The Queen Anne's Revenge sleeps idly. She has not been careened in months and probably should have been six times in such.

I am happy to say that I have performed no ceremonies but this only shows how far his passions have fallen. He did nothing but drink gallons of rum and smoke opiate-soaked tobacco. The more I was away from him, the more I missed him. We all to often allow time to soften the turmoil that one has put us through only replace it with embellished, fond memories.

Return Of The King

February 21st, 1718. I sat alone in my cabin. I have not lifted a plume in over a week. I missed it but I too had lost a part of myself, just as Blackbeard had. My limited exposure to smoking the devilish cocktail had taken its toll on me.

Back on the ship, I would find myself wanting it more and more. Being just outside of the village was good for me. I had less access to the things that could harm me. The Rio Grande do Sul was a small place that saw a lot of traffic. In some ways, it reminded me of Bath. I missed home. I missed my family. Through my writings, I hope that I have given them peace.

Both of the cats from the ship had taken residence with me. After about three weeks of being left aboard The Queen Anne's Revenge, I realized that they must surely be running low on rats. Each night, they would come to sit at my feet as I dined and would collect all the unwanted portions.

The shelves were low on food but it was not due to any financial strain. We were all very well taken care of and I had spent far less money than anyone else. I had simply become lazy. I had finally visited the market today and was expecting a visit from Gorma at any time. He owned the small store and would be bringing me a delivery at any point now.

Since landing here, I had begun to learn a bit of Portuguese. I still enjoyed reading but most anything I could find was left over from the missions. It was limited but still something enjoyable. My time here has allowed me to come into my own and feel to be an adult.

I awoke each day and prepared my meals. I did my own shopping and I cleaned the home. I paid my own debts and most importantly, I had broken myself of the Devil's addiction.

There was a knock at the door and I quickly announced that it was ok to come in. A young native boy opened it and I could see his wooden cart just outside. It was filled with goods of all types. He quickly brought mine in and placed them on the table. He was most likely no more than ten or eleven and was extremely small. Most of the locals were. As tiny as my frame was often considered, he was smaller. His hair was cut into a bowl-like shape and was shaved bald on top. While different than I was *accustomed, I found nothing odd anymore.*

I thanked him with the hopes that he understood. I had already paid for the goods earlier but I also always offered the locals gratuity for many things in which they did. I signaled for him to stay where he stood and I went to the bedroom to fetch his coinage.

As I counted out five pieces for him, I heard him speak loudly to me. "Apresse-se senhora. Alguém está aqui!" His voice seemed to have a slight bit of fear in it; although he was not in a full-blown panic. With embarrassment, I did not understand what he was saying. I had become much better at slowly reading other languages rather than translating quick bursts. When I went back into the main room, my jaw dropped. It was Blackbeard. There he stood in my doorway. He was a skeleton; a shell of the man I once knew.

"Laddy, we need to talk. May I sit?"

"Yes. Yes, of course, you can!" I quickly pulled a chair out from the table for him. I then handed the young man his coinage and motioned him in a way that he knew I was safe. He left.

"Laddy, you seemed to have found your weight once more."

"Yes, yes I have gladly. I have been eating well and taking much better care of myself." As I stood across to him, I could notice that he now had a gold tooth on the top and to his left side. I did not ask why he needed such a thing. The call for it would have only been more shocking.

"I think I am dying, Laddy. Could the devil have lied to me? We had a deal. This sickness that has taken its hold on me. It seems the work of evil."

"I cannot attest to it being evil or of other doing but I can cure you. I know its origins. I too have battled it. And I whipped it."

"You have beaten this dark sickness? Are you sure? There are several other men that seem to have it as well. None of which have fared well against it."

"Your enemy is your nightlife."

"What say you?"

"It is the very life in which you have chosen that has caused your pain. You never eat. You drink like a fish. You smoke that wretched oil several times a day. This is the source of your malaise."

"*Your stupidity never fades, does it? I thought you were going to help me. You aim to let me die, bitch!*"

"*No, I do not aim to let you die. I aim to help you. I joined this crew to write of its journey and yet, the journey has ended. You do nothing anymore but feed those things in which I just mentioned. Think about the words I say. It's true. You are not a pirate anymore. You do nothing and you will soon be broke. And then . . .*"

"*I am broke.*"

"*What???*"

"*I am now broke. Completely broke. I have nothing. The ships are empty. My pockets are empty. I have nothing.*"

"*That is not true. You have me. Let me do what it is I was hired to do. Let me tell the world of how brilliant you are.*"

"*Yes laddy, you're right! I will tell the crew that we sail tomorrow morning! Pack your belongings!*"

"*No. I choose not to go. Not like this.*"

"*Why? Your words have no meaning! Is this what*

you are saying to me?"

"You are not well and if I go, you will make me ill once more. If you wish me to go, you must cure yourself first. If you wish to depart tomorrow morning, then do so with my blessing but know that I will not be by your side."

"Your answer to this?"

"If you, Blackbeard, wish to truly embark on the most daring of journeys, you will show up here tomorrow morning."

"And? Are you a witch? You will magically cure me of the devil's illness?"

"In a sort? Yes. But most importantly, you will cure yourself. You will beat back the greatest demon a man could ever face. I will be here to help. It will not be easy. You will learn to hate me more than you have thought possible. And at the end of this all, perhaps you will find yourself again."

"Why wait, laddy? Perform your magic now."

"No. Go out tonight. Live your life and do as you please. Tell the crew that you are going on a personal homage. This homage will last two weeks. Do not tell them

where you are going or why you are doing it. Implicitly direct them to not seek your whereabouts; for you do not wish to be found."

"Two weeks! What sense does this make???"

"For a man that feels he has no time left, two weeks cannot be argued. You will either be here tomorrow morning and follow my exact instructions, or you won't."

* * * * * * * * *

I had no idea if he would show or not. There were parts of me that hoped for either outcome. I had nothing to win with him showing and nothing to lose. His tone was questionable last night but still with heavy interest. He did not need me to know what shape he was in. He was in a tattered sort.

I can only imagine that if he truly did plan on coming, he would be in a rugged manner. Knowing it will be your last night without something in which you are so attached would mean he might drown himself in it prior.

I sat out front and enjoyed a delicious melon for breakfast. I watched The Queen Anne's Revenge sit afar on the horizon with no purpose. While she was still afloat, I could not see her being seaworthy within a year. The hull had been neglected for far too long. It would be his own fault if she sank and killed us all one day. The Tree of Woe and The Revenge have both seen the maintenance and care they required multiple times. He simply needed to have given the orders and it would have been done, but he did not.

As I tossed the rinds of my last bit of fruit to the side, I spied him wandering toward me. I watched him stagger and I watched him fall. One could not be sure if it were the rum or opiate that caused his most current state but I had the cures for him no matter.

I opened my front door and with no words still, he walked in. His head was hung low and I could barely see his face under his hair and beard. His smell was wretched. Then, he looked up at me and finally spoke.

"Well, let it begin. What will you have me do?"

"For now, all you must do is drink."

"Just drink, laddy? This will not be a problem."

I pointed to the bed in the corner of my bedroom. "Sit. There is a large bottle of rum on the table beside the bed. Use the glass that I have left for you. In it, you will find a powder. It will mix with your rum and let you rest. When you leave this room, you will be well."

"And where will you be sleeping?"

"There are accommodations for me in the other room. I will be fine. Trust my words, you should not be worried about my well being right now. Yours is that of question."

He did as I asked with no further comments which only added to how deeply his own desperation must run right now. He poured the entire glass down as if it were his last, then he made himself another.

"Ok Sir, two glasses will be enough. This fix had the powder in it. That is all that you need."

"It helped me sleep."

"You will have no issues with sleep. This, I assure you."

****

I was in the other room when it began. I heard the

rattling sound coming from his room. It was immediately followed by his loud outcry. "You fucking bitch!!! What have you done to me??? Laddy!!! Get your arse in here now!!! I am going to fucking kill you!!!"

I crept slowly to the doorway and peeped in. He was securely tied in place to each bedpost with heavy, leather lashings. I knew that he was secure but still, I was petrified. He told no lies in the fact that if freed, he would kill me. I slowly entered.

"Good morning, Sir."

"Good morning??? Do not dare greet me with such soft cadence!!! You are holding me hostage! I am going to kill you and kill you slowly!!!"

"Now listen to me. I am only helping you. You cannot beat this demon on your own. It simply is not possible."

"Go to Hell, you bitch!!! Do not tell me what I am capable of! I do not believe for one goddamn moment that you were tied down and incapacitated for two weeks to overcome this menace." His voice calmed slightly.

"No. No, I was not but I was not nearly as burdened with the illness as you. And even still, I suffered

horribly. You will eventually see splitting headaches, chills, fevers and sweats, body soreness. You are going to feel like you are dying."

"Thank you for lining the way with positive wishes. What time is it? How long have I been here? How long was I asleep?"

I did not want to further anger him but I also know he would relentlessly question me until he had answers. I hesitated for a moment but his stare would not falter. "Well, you have been here for three days."

"Three goddamn days!" He looked down at his body and feet. He was covered with a thin blanket but soon come to realize that he was not dressed in the way that he had arrived. "Am I naked? I smell like oils. Did you also bathe me???"

"Wait. Just relax. You were filthy when you arrived. I simply took care of you. There is no other way."

He looked upward at his wrists and his confines, quickly testing them with a couple hard tugs and then stared at me once more. "Let me go now, you miserable bitch. I swear before all that I know that I will kill you at the first chance I get."

"You cannot do such and you know this. It will break your pact. Trust me, I know that you are in pain right now. It will get better; this I declare to you. But before you know any peace, it will get worse. Much worse."

"Well I have needs that must be attended and this cannot wait."

"Yes, I realize this. Your chamber pot is here, beside the bed."

"So then, you will free me long enough to handle my affairs, correct? Tell me that you will at least afford me this bit of decency?"

"Yes. Yes, Sir, I will. But first, you must drink your rum again."

"What? You will repeat this to me again and again?"

"Yes. Yes, Sir, I will. You will drink your rum and have some fresh, clean water with a tray of fruit I have for you. Once done, I will free your legs and one of your hand. By this time, you will only have moments. Use them wisely. Handle your private affairs and lay back down. If not, I will find you on the floor and I do not know

that I have the strength to lift you. Do you understand?"

"Do not order me, bitch! Yes, I understand."

* * * * * * * * *

He slept even longer this time. Yesterday, I feared that he had died. His heartbeat has grown faint and weak. I do not know anymore if I am doing the right thing for him. He may have been too far into this sickness when we began. Under my methods, he is getting barely any food or water and once he arises again, the real pain will have set in.

On more than one occasion, he had vomited on himself and nearly choked. He would never know the ways I had chosen to care for him while he was in slumber. The first two days, he soaked and soiled himself to no end. Tomorrow, I would be adding leeches to help draw out the illness. In speaking to an elder nearby, he has promised that this would help.

It was the seventh day of his treatment and I prayed that he would awake. I began by trimming his fingernails and then on to his feet. I trimmed up the ends of his hair and beard as it had become tattered in appearance. After bathing him, I covered him in wet

towels and opened the windows to cool his body. The
sweats had found him and had him fiery to the touch. His
breath filled the room with the smell of death so I placed
mint gel in his mouth and I placed balm on his scabby
lips.

His ribs were countable and I knew that he needed
more than just fruit. I kept pieces of bread and wine
nearby in the expectation that he would speak today. I had
honey on standby as well as I knew this would give him
fresh life if anything would.

His eyes were matted with sickness so I cleaned
them so. I changed his earrings with some I found at the
market. They were made of silver and more fitting than
the wooden ones he had in. Then, I braided his beard and
tied ribbons into each end. The better he looked, the better
he would feel. Perhaps this was my silly way of
convincing myself that I was helping him to get better.

When he finally came to, he was not the beast of
wrath and revenge as he was the first time. He was weak
and groggy. He mumbled through his words which were
largely not of any language I knew. He could be speaking
one of the many tongues he knew or he could simply not
have his mind.

Being at least partially awake, I knew that this

was my best chance to get food into him. He should be able to chew and swallow. I began by soaking his bread in honey and giving him very small pieces. He was receptive and the more I fed him, the more he seemed to crave. I lifted his head and placed a second pillow underneath to prop him up higher. This too was very helpful. After each bite, I would alternate giving him wine and water. Soon, the bread and honey were both gone so I gently pressed a plantain into mush and he quickly ate that as well. He was going to survive this thing. He could not die. He slept with Lucifer's protection.

****

I gave him less and less sleeping powder during the last few days. On day twelve, his chills had broken. He had been shown himself in the mirror and seemed to be pleased; thankful even. I still took great care to watch myself around him. He was a snake and I knew that it could all easily be a ploy to get free or to get his hands around my throat.

Still, though, I would keep my promise. On the fifteenth day, I went into his room and he was already awake. He looked at me and smiled. Although he was still a thin version of who he was months ago, he had regained his color, his skin looked better and his voice had regained *its deep, dominant tone.*

"Laddy, will you do as you have said? Is today not the day that I am to be free?"

"Do not think of yourself as being free from me. Think of yourself as being free from the illness."

"I have been nothing but cruel to you. Why would you dare to help me? And before you answer, do not say that it is because you love me. There is more."

"I do love you . . . and yes, there is more; much more. I have beaten my demons but I cannot be around you if you do not beat your own. Those with the sickness thrive from being with others that share it. You have now beaten yours and you have a much tougher decision to make. You must look at your crew and tell them that it is not to ever be aboard The Queen Anne's Revenge ever again."

"What? That is insane. Men join this lifestyle to seek freedom. If I were to run my ship and crew in such a manner, I would be no better than a Royal Navy Commander. That is something that I am not and have no desire to be."

"Do not worry, they will not stop. But they will see

that you do not wish to be around it or exposed to it. If either of us is placed in its path, we will fail. If you stay clear of it, you will become history's greatest pirate. They will throw carnivals in celebration of your name and conquests. You will live forever."

"You sound so inspirational, Laddy. How many times have you uttered that speech to yourself?"

"Too many. But every word is true. By the way, I have more for you. I am going to remove your shackles now. Please do not kill me." I slowly freed each ankle and then his wrists. He rubbed each spot where the lashings were and rightfully so. They were raw even though I had treated them with healing balm. He slowly stood and took his balance. I reached into the armoire and sat several items on the bed.

"What are these, laddy?"

"New attire for you. I had them custom made. You have new boots as well. Every item; all black. Your boots are from black caiman. You will look the part you are fulfilling."

"Where did you get the money for these. The quality is astounding."

"I did not waste my money on the illness. You deserve these. I have eight total here for you. Now, go claim your crew, Blackbeard."

* * * * * * * * *

It was a beautiful morning and the first in some time where I had felt that familiar breeze. The salt tasted great on my lips and the sun warmed my skin as only it could. I stood behind him under the mast and for the first time, I felt that he was proud to have me by his side.

Umar was to my left. He stood just as proudly and I believed that he too was proud of the new direction that The Queen Anne's Revenge had taken, both geographically and spiritually. There were several members that did not join us on our new mission and instead, decided to stay behind and live with their demons. As we pulled to a place that put the Brazilian coastline out of site for good, Umar asked our reborn captain of our future. He pushed his chest outward and replied.

"Point us North, dear friend. We are headed back to The English Colonies. Those banks are my home and I never intend to leave them again. On our journey, we will meet three types of ships. The first will be ships of war. Any official Navy vessel you meet, I want you to destroy.

The second will be fellow pirates and privateers. Those will be asked to align with us and grow our armada. The third will be the merchant ship. These are our lifeline. Pillage everything you see without exception."

The Siege Of Charles Towne

March 31st, 1718. It was early. There was no sun visible yet but the sky was beautifully lit. Ambera had thrown the flag of attack and darted out ahead of The Queen Anne's Revenge and Stede Bonnet's ship, The Revenge had joined her.

Through the spyglass, I could see three ships that appeared to be huddled together. We were nearly in Spanish Floridian waters and had taken 30 ships in only a couple weeks. It had become common with our raids that as the action was spotted, our two faster ships in the fleet would dart ahead.

By pure design, The Queen Anne's Revenge is a large, heavy ship. The sloops that sailed by our sides were naturally faster. But we had all noticed that our flagship had become much slower. It had been another lifetime since she had been properly careened. Umar said only days earlier that she handled as if her weight had doubled.

Add to that the takings of loot from many other ships and we had become very cumbersome. He even secretly feared that she would fall apart asea one day.

As we closed in on the encounter, Ambera and Bonnet had nearly reached the three ships that were originally huddled. It appeared that we had come upon another piratic raid in progress. The Tree Of Woe sent grappling hooks across first as always.

We could see that she was not in attack mode and Ambera had not yet been sent hurling through the morning air. The attack flags had been dropped and all parties seemed to be crossing ships amicably. Finally, we arrived. Myself, Umar, and Blackbeard boarded the center ship.

There, we found Bonnet and his right-hand, Anne-Catherine & Ambera McDaniels, and another pirate captain huddled around in conversation. He was tall and very muscular; broadly shouldered. He may have had the biggest chest and arms that I have ever witnessed. He was clean shaven and square-jawed with coarse, black hair that was very tightly and very neatly pulled back into a ponytail. His clothing was neat and his low cut shoes were shiny. He may have been chiseled from stone. His voice was almost perfectly annoying but it had a playful, Gaelic accent to it. This bold figure jumped out and spoke to him first with a handshake extended.

He stumbled over his own words and thoughts. "Ahhhh, the famous and notorious Blackbeard. I have heard nothing but bad things! Bad things are good things of course because we are pirates. Of course, you know that we are pirates. You are a great pirate. And with being a great pirate, that means bad. Not that you are bad at it but that you do bad things."

Blackbeard cut off his rambling quickly. "Please, I understand. Your name is?"

"I, Sir am William Lee Graddy the Third. Don't let the third be my rank. For I am first in everything. I am only the third based on the name in which my parents chose to call me and . . . "

Blackbeard quickly ended his sharp, Irish chatter. "I understand quite well how names work." Graddy smiled with the playfulness of a three-year-old.

Ambera interjected herself into the talks. "Our high-energy friend here would like to join the fleet of Blackbeard."

"You can swear allegiance to me here and now?"

"Oh Sir, not only can I swear allegiance, I can bring your fleet to new levels and heights." The chatterbox started his powerful roll once more. "I can bring you to such heights that . . . "

"Relax, relax, relax. I am going to take this as a Yes. Shall we shake . . . a silent handshake?" Blackbeard smiled.

"Yes Sir, I am the king of being silent. All pirates have nicknames now and I am quite surprised that I have not yet been penned as Silent Will or Silent Willy Lee, or Silent William the third. Of course, the third would not really apply because although I am the third, my father and grandfather were not referred to as silent so I am actually the first."

Blackbeard eyed him with a serious gaze. "How do you keep such fervor, I must ask?"

The Irishman seemed to be excited to answer and with each word, his pace became faster. "Well I am naturally one to be active in conversations as such but now I have discovered the magic of coca leaves? I chew them constantly. Have you ever heard of such? Of course, you have, for you are as worldly as I if not more. Speaking of worldly, I have heard of your exploits in the French seas to the north. Imagine what you could do via doubling your fleet size. Here I arrived with two ships and captured a third. Then through fortuitous design, your three find my three and we become six. The funny thing about the number six is . . ."

"Whoa!!! I need you to breathe. I fear your heart may stop before we get to work together."

The mighty Irishman grabbed me and began pressing me over his head before I even knew what was happening. "Sir, my heart is in no danger. I am fit as a fig and strong as any oxen you have seen. Is there something else that I can lift?" Without stoppage in his speech, he gently tossed me to the side and grabbed a powder keg. This thing must have weighed three of me. "See? I tell you that I am more than any four men could handle; five even. Other than you. Not that you are not a man. You are not just any man though. You are Blackbeard! Not that you do not know who you are. You seem to have your wits about you and I can imagine . . ."

"Stop!!! Place the explosive keg down, please. Welcome to our armada. You will be a powerful ally."

Graddy gave a boyish smile and did something that I have never witnessed anyone do before. He grabbed the lanky Blackbeard and hugged him in quite the manly embrace. As Graddy had his eyes closed in elation, his *captive looked to Anne-Catherine and me in hopes that he would soon be freed from his awkward embrace. Ambera chuckled and patted Teach on his shoulder as she walked away. From more than ten feet away, she playfully yelled. "You're welcome, Blackbeard!"*

* * * * * * * * * *

We had only been back in motion for about four hours but we were making great time. The northern current was with us and the wind had joined the effort. This was a good thing for our massive ship.

Our fleet was now an incredible force. I was sure to record each captain and ship name for the logs. To the far left and slightly ahead of all was Ambera and Anne-Catherine on The Tree Of Woe.

Just beside them was Stede Bonnet, The Gentleman Pirate and his sloop, The Revenge. In the center and afront was the wild Irishman that I had jokingly called Chatty Graddy but he was logged as he requested, William Lee Graddy the Third. He was sailing his Class III gunner that was named The Menacing Meagan.

The other ship that joined us via his agreement

was captained by Graddy's best friend and trusted partner, Anthony Wrenn. Wrenn was the exact opposite of Graddy in every way but also a perfect counterpart. Wrenn had his blonde hair shaved closely and was diabolically quiet. He studied everything. He was leading an eighteen-gun sloop called The Ungood.

Off to the far right was the ship that Graddy had taken this morning when we came upon him. Blackbeard placed his own trusted friend, Israel Hands to lead her. He was better known in the piracy world as Basilica Hands and he sailed The Adventure. The captain that was sailing it at the time of the taking was Captain Herriot and he had chosen to join us as well.

Sixth and finally, there was our own ship. The Queen Anne's Revenge sent guns to our new partners this morning but still had 28 powerful cannons that were primed for battle. All in all, across the armada, there were now over 700 of us at my best count. We may truly be the most powerful unit in the seas including military powers for hundreds of miles in every direction.

* * * * * * * * *

The sun created their silhouettes at a time that they may have otherwise gone unnoticed. Ambera once again spotted them first and threw up her flags. She and Bonnet broke loose and the rest of us would follow closely.

By the time we reached the southbound travelers on our trek north, we realized that they were eight deep and not running. They all turned broadside and created a wall of destruction from the time we were a half mile away. This is when we found out how important Graddy and Wrenn would be to our cause.

Without saying, every ship involved in piracy, privateering, or the defense thereof needed gunpowder and tons of it. We all generally used it in the same manner; these two, however, did things differently. As we neared, their two ships used catapults to fire what we could only figure to be the entire kegs and they had been wick lit for the launch. When they made contact, they exploded and the entire ship went up in flames. Before we could make sense of the situation, there were now three ships that were nothing more than burning pyres afloat in the sea.

Their crews began to jump overboard. Many were already lifeless, floating bodies. Quickly, the rest hoisted flags of surrender and welcomed our boarding. As the grappling hooks went over, the crews pulled the ships together. Within moments, we were being loaded with an abundance of goods that were very valuable and in this case, also needed for our large, floating city.

This is where things began to take an ominous turn. As crews surrendered, it was the unwritten rule that the aggressors would allow their survival. But one by one, Wrenn and Graddy began to slash the frightened and confused sailors and tossing their bodies into the ocean.

Blackbeard neither gave the commands for this to happen or to stop it. Rather, he watched on without opinion and simply allowed it to happen. Within moments, all eight ships were in blazes, hundreds were dead, and we were adding to the legacy of our namesake. Things of this nature certainly made my job easier.

* * * * * * * * *

I sat in my cabin and more closely detailed the events of today. Within mere hours, we had grown from 300 men to more than twice such. We became a six-ship armada when only three left the sands not long ago. We were completely replenished in our need for new supplies and weapons, and most importantly, we found our souls and purpose.

As midnight appeared, I wondered if he would start back. Would Satan call to him to council once more?

I could always tell when he had used opiates before because it would keep him from snoring. If he snored, he had not used but if he lay in a dead slumber after smoking it, his breaths would become shallow and too weak to muster a sound.

Tonight, he would once again make me proud. He came in before midnight and only moments later, his candles fell dark. At this point, we would all be asleep within minutes. This day was an exciting, exhausted blur.

* * * * * * * * * *

I heard him early that morning. He was in agony. I kept quiet at first because I did not know the nature of his discomfort.   As I sat and listened, I could tell this was ongoing. As easily as possible, I made my way to the curtain and opened the smallest of slits in the doorway. His next sound became that of a wild boar being deballed. There was no doubt that the crew may have heard such a calling.

When I yanked the curtain back, I found him with his trousers on the floor and hovering over his chamber pot. It was apparent that he was trying to relieve himself but I did not know at first of what method. Whatever the source of his pain, it was more than enough to allow this to bypass any embarrassment and beg for help.

"Laddy!!! This is killing me!!!" He collapsed back on his cot and he was fully exposed. I have never seen such a site. His entire private area was covered in large blisters and he appeared to be oozing some sort of blood mixture from his manhood. I looked down at the chamber pot and it had blood in it.

I sat down beside him and pulled a sheet over his unhealthiness. "What is this ailment? Were you injured in today's battle somehow? Burned maybe?"

"No Laddy, this is The French Disease. It is most likely of my own doing. God has punished me for my sins."

"Yes, God did this for my matrimonial betrayals. I am sure of this. He and Satan play the most sadistic of games. God forces me to live with this pain and The Devil won't let me die. I just have a life of pain promised to me."

"Well, there has to be a treatment. Leeches maybe?"

"No. No leech can draw this out. The French Disease attacks your soul. This sickness has settled within one of the body's Four Humors. Are you aware of these?" He grimaced.

"Yes, you forget I am well read. The Four Humors are Yellow Bile, Blood, Black Bile, and Phlegm. Which do you believe has been affected?"

"This is a problem of more than one; this is my fear. However, there is a cure according to experts. Back in Bath Towne, Daniel Ferrell once spoke of a treatment."

"And this is?"

"A night with Venus; a lifetime of Mercury."

"So then, if we get your Mercury, you will be cured. Well then, we must make haste. We can be ashore on the mainland in a couple days. Surely they will have what you need."

"Not just anyone has Mercury. We must sail to Charles Towne."

"Charles Towne is too dangerous for pirates. You know this. This whole area below The Cape of Fear straight down to Spanish Florida had been declared off limits to all privateers. Sir, I beg of you another option. Can we not at least try?"

"No. And I want to keep this a secret. When we get to Charles Towne, I know a way to get what it is I need with privacy, etch my name in the stones of history, and make the stop most bountiful."

* * * * * * * * *

We arrived off the shores of Charles Towne on May 21st, 1718. It was well before dawn. He ordered us to wake him upon arrival. He went to the bow and gave a signal to the others that I had not seen before. In half an hour, our armada had stretched across The Port of Charles Towne and we had enacted a blockade. Little did we know that this act would eventually become one of history's most infamous acts and we were led here all because of his deformed penis.

Daylight came and it was early when The Province of South Carolina sent out messengers to officially represent the Governor. This was unheard of and they seemed willing to do anything to put it to an end.

We placed a roundtable on the bow as we always did when there would be such a gathering. At the table, I

*felt as if I was sitting with The Gods; perhaps I was.
There were Ambera, Anne-Catherine, Wrenn, Graddy,
Hands, Blackbeard, Ellis the scribe, Bonnet, and several
South Carolinian representatives.*

*One of the well-dressed spokesmen started. "I sit
here with you privateers today to expedite your removal.
Charles Towne nor any town, port, or dwelling within the
South Carolina Provence will tolerate your livelihood
here."*

*Graddy and Wrenn removed their sabres in
tandem and pressed the point against his throat. Chatty
Graddy looked to Blackbeard with enthusiasm. "Shall I
kill him, Sir?"*

"No, not yet."

*"But Commodore Blackbeard, I want his shoes. I
ask again, may I kill him?"*

*"No, not yet. Sir, remove your shoes and give them
to my friend now please."*

"My shoes? Are you mad?"

*Ambera pulled a dagger quickly and added it to
his neck which was quickly becoming a pin cushion.*

"Remove your shoes and knickers. Any arguments will quickly become more embarrassing for you."

"I will do no such. You heathens can afford your own shoes and knickers!"

Wrenn grabbed him from behind by his ponytail and stood him up violently. With only one low whisper in his ear, he uttered. "Disrobe."

The man knew that this would not end. He removed everything but his bottom undergarment and stood there as the group smiled. Ambera grabbed the remaining clothes on each side of his hip and yanked them to the ground. The man quickly covered his genitals and the group laughed.

Graddy reached down and placed the man's shoe beside his own only to find out that they were going to be far too small to fit. Graddy quickly grabbed the man's ponytail in anger and led him to the edge of The Queen Anne's Revenge and tossed him over. "The bastard tried to trick me!"

Blackbeard slowly leaned across the table to the other two officials and spoke. "Do you now realize that this is not a negotiation?"

"Yes!" "Yes, Sir" Both were in complete compliance.

"Good. Now, this is how this is going to work. We are going to sit here for as long as we like. Any ship that tries to pass will be ours without exception."

One of the officials nervously spoke. "Sir, we will gladly relay your message. We are only here as a mouthpiece. I must warn that there is a close alliance between South Carolina and Virginia. The governor has already sent word that we are in need of Naval assistance. You should leave now. Go to North Carolina where you are welcomed."

"I will stay here for as long as I like."

"Well Sir Blackbeard, what is it that you seek? Perhaps we can persuade the governor to quickly meet your demands. We simply want to trade and commerce to commence quickly and with no port, we cannot do such."

"I will send two small boats to the mainland this afternoon. They will fill both boats with all medications, drugs, and remedies that you have. This must include Mercury in the forms of both ointments and pills. No exceptions."

"But to fill both of those crafts will take weeks!"

The group began to look inquisitive to demand. I felt that I needed to serve their suspicion. I quickly interjected. "We have buyers awaiting these precious supplies so I would suggest you act now before they arrive also. Go!"

The group jumped up with urgency. It felt so good for my words to hold this power. As they walked away, Blackbeard placed his hand on my shoulder. I knew that he was proud of me even if he would never say as much.

As they began to row away, I could see that the naked man had climbed into the craft with the rest. I looked down at his clothing and realized that they may fit me, so I took them with me down below.

****

Before dark, both men left with a list of goods to locate and bring back. They were told not to return until all were aboard and as much as possible.

Later that night, I decided to walk the deck. I noticed something large moving across the water against the treeline. I grabbed the bell and rang it quickly. Umar was the first to show. As he ran up, I pointed it out to him. He stared for a moment and I knew that he could see it too.

He blew a horn three times. I knew that there were specifics in this that I did not understand. In only a minute, lanterns were abound on The Tree Of Woe and The Revenge. Both ships were darting across the expanse at a pace that we could have only hoped to have moved.

Blackbeard came up and stood beside me. "What is it, Laddy?"

"I saw something trying to slip by us."

Umar replied. "He did, Sir. His young eyes are far more than my own. Even after shown, it took me a moment to see her . . . but she's there."

Once again, Blackbeard was proud of me and though it was not spoken, it was in his voice. "Very good, Laddy. It will be interesting to find what was so important that they risk to slip it past us."

****

Within an hour, the ship made its way to our own.

Bonnet steered the vessel up close and brought prisoners aboard. Before talks could begin, another craft was seen moving through the waterway and it too was attacked. While its goods were being pirated, Blackbeard spoke to those brought on board.

"So, why would you people seek to take such risks? If you meet my demands, you would be rid of me in the blink of an eye. And yet stupidly, here you are."

One of the men stepped forward in anger. "You cannot do this! Have you no idea who I am??? You ignorant scalliwag, you will hang for this!!!"

"No, I have no idea who you are. The question is, do you know who I am?"

"Yes, I know who you are. You are Blackbeard. Let me tell you now that you are a wanted man in these seas and you will hang! Listen closely to these words. I am Samuel Wragg and you have captured The Crowley! I am a member of South Carolina's Council. You have sentenced yourself to a noose!"

"So, I have a councilman? Interesting. Do you reckon that you are of value to the people? Politicians are something that I see no value in. Perhaps I should test this, no?"

"You are only testing your time here. Free my family and I this very moment and I will let you live!"

Blackbeard grabbed the man by the throat and lifted him against the wall, holding him in place. His small children and wife began to cry and beg for life. He moved in, eye to eye. "If you ever threaten me again, I will skin your children here as you watch. Do you understand me?"

"Yes."

"Loudly! I cannot hear you. Do you understand me, you miserable piece of shite???"

"I understand completely. Just let my children be."

****

Five days had passed and our men had not returned. No coinage, no money, no supplies, and no medication had been brought to The Queen Anne's Revenge. We realized that it may take a couple days, perhaps more to gather the amounts that they had been charged with but by now, we knew something was wrong.

"*Laddy! Get here now. I need two documents written. Bring your quill and papers.*"

I rushed up to the levels where he stood and asked him of his needs.

"*The first one is to The Charles Towne Council. It should read as follows:*

Dear Council of Charles Towne,

I have tried to be fair with you weasels and you have betrayed my trust. I made a list of demands and you have sent nothing. I have stated that I would kill the hostages on this day and I have been lenient thus far. I have asked that no ships approach and we have now raided more than a dozen offenders. I am sending my scribe along with two others. If he has not returned to me by tomorrow evening, I will march 700 of my men your way and Charles Towne will burn.

Sincerely, Commodore Blackbeard
PS: Kiss my hairy arse."

"*I have it all, Sir, word for word. Now, you are sending me?*"

"*Yes, I need you to see that things are going as I*

wish. I am not able to make the trip. Today is not a good day for me. Please privately bring me the medications I need, even if it is just a small portion. I am not well."

"Yes Sir, I will. You asked for two letters. To whom would the next be sent and what is its message?"

"The next will be sent to Virginia, for Governor Alexander Spotswood."

"I have it, Sir. And the message?"

"Two words, only two, Laddy."

"And they are?'

"I'm coming."

* * * * * * * * *

I sat with Robin Hood and Leland as they rowed the boat inland. I was nervous admittedly and I believe that my partners were as well. We had no idea what had been done to our previous team or if the same fate awaited us. The trip was long and it took half the day to make it to the banks. As we neared the banks, we were shocked at what we found.

There sat our two boats; there sat our crew. Both were safe. They were laid out on the docks; rum in hand and they were all but asleep. Umar came out of our ship in anger.

"What is the matter with you idiots??? We have been waiting for days for you to arrive with those goods!!! We are holding hostages that could have been killed because of you!!! A naval fleet near us every single day and here we await while you lay on the pier and just drink and sleep!!! I should kill you now!!!"

They did not move. This was more than just alcohol. I did not know what they had found to use but it was more than they could handle. In the water beside them floated hundreds of vials of medication. I could even see the much needed Mercury that was so very wanted by our leader.

With the paddles, Leland and I began to push the floating medications to the edge and gather them together. We placed them in the supply boat and tried to assure that we had everything. As I lifted the oar up and looked closely, it appeared to be covered in a thick red tint. It was blood. I quickly turned around to realize that Umar had sliced the throats of those that had failed him. We would quickly get these items back to our armada and The Siege of Charles Towne would finally come to an end.

High And Dry

June 2nd, 1718. Once the goods that we asked for in Charles Towne were collected, we freed the prisoners and departed as quickly as possible. We knew that while there were much more reapings to be had in such a majestic town, we had also more than worn out our welcome.

Both South Carolina and Virginia had decreed the year before to end piracy or privateering of any kind in their waters. Alexander Spotswood from Virginia had already called both Blackbeard and Bonnet by name in multiple publications and as those two sought fame for piracy, the governor sought fame for ending it.

The relationship between the English Colonies could be odd and stretched at times. Commerce existed in bountiful amounts between them all and was a much-needed force. However, those that make the deals within the trade were often corrupt.

Politicians and business owners would strike a

trade deal and then insure it only to contact a pirate or privateer to attack it and give them a portion of the proceeds so that they would be able to claim some of their goods or funds back as well as the insurance settlements. No more was this a problem than in North Carolina.

Both South Carolina and Virginia did plenty of good business in North Carolina and obviously traveled both its land and seas. But it was also well known that North Carolina was in support and in cahoots with highwaymen on the land and piracy asea. This direct connection ran all the way up to the governor of North Carolina himself, Governor Eden.

Blackbeard, Bonnet, and all of our leaders knew this as well. Therefore, The Port of Charles Towne would no longer be a safe place for us. Not only did we pirate nearly a dozen ships and hold an important citizen and his family captive, we ran a blockade of the entire town. This was unheard of on this level. We must get to North Carolina and do so quickly.

Once on open waters, it became very obvious as to how slow The Queen Anne's Revenge had become. The entire fleet had to wait for her to keep up and it was only worsening. At times, the behemoth was barely moving at all and felt anchored. Tensions within the group between captains were starting to grow. This became most *apparent between Blackbeard and Bonnet.*

We could see Bonnet and two of his men paddling their way to The Queen Anne's Revenge and he seemed to be angered from 100 yards away. Before their craft had even reached the edge well, Stede was standing and ready to grab the ladder netting. He could not get aboard quickly enough.

As soon as he crossed over the ledge, he was stomping our way with emotion and direction. I stood close by Blackbeard unknowing if he would hear him out or knock him unconscious.

"Ahhhhh, it's Stede Bonnet. The Gentleman Pirate. You are here to act as a gentleman, I would assume?"

"You are going to send us straight to the gallows if you cannot get this ship moving any faster!"

"Relax, we will have reached The Cape of Fear in another day and that will place us in North Carolina waters."

"Do not dare try to teach me geometry and trajectory! I know where we are and where we are headed. What I fail to understand is why this ship, which was

once a fine vessel might I have you, is now no more than a slug and a thorn in my side???"

As he finished his tirade, Blackbeard stuffed a couple coca leaves into his gums and smiled as he listened.

Bonnet seemed even more steamed now. "What??? You are using coca again!!!"

Blackbeard then removed his pipe from the quiver in his hat that held it and placed three or four opiate drops in its basin with the tobacco. Everyone knew what the drops were. I must admit that I too was heartbroken but I would never publicly chastise him in this way. Bonnet however chose to continue.

"You, Edward Teach are a disgrace to piracy and will end up being the reason for failure in what would have otherwise have become an empire! Your addictions are a sign of weakness. You have no self-control!"

Blackbeard stepped closer as he realized that they had captured every eye of the crew. "Choose your words wisely, Bonnet."

"Do not threaten me, Edward. Many of these men were mine first and would gladly take your head if I requested. Do not forget such."

"Is that a fact? Well, Stede . . . what you may not realize is that most of those same men came to me and asked me to take over your business. Your piracy skills were so bad that they were ready to toss you over and name a new captain." Bonnet went to turn away and Blackbeard grabbed his arm. "Stede, listen to me. I am being serious with you. They were ready to kill you. I saved you. I will not do it again."

"Do you think I owe you??? Edward, even if I do, I should not have to repay you with my life!!! If we are caught here, that will be our cost."

"I cannot force the winds to blow any harder. What do you suggest, Gentlemanly Pirate?"

"I suggest that the moment we are safely and well within North Carolina, you careen your ship! It may take a week or more to remove the abuse you have allowed to collect on her. But more importantly, do not allow your stupid addictions to let your ship become what it has!!!"

"I will live my life as I please and I suggest you do the same with none of your business to mesh with mine. You are not perfect, Bonnet."

"I have claimed no level of perfection, but I have

claimed self-control. This is something that you cannot."

"I have heard enough of your petty lectures. I have a solution to our problem. We will lock our ships together and unload all of the heavy cargo onto the other lighter ships. You must remember how much bounty there is down below us. I'll have all of the gold and coinage loaded onto your craft. Our crews, supplies, and food will go aboard the remaining ships. This will raise the hull setting for The Queen Anne's Revenge and I will sail her with a skeleton crew into Beaufort Inlet by Topsail. There, she will get a proper careening."

"Fine, that will solve our immediate problem but that does not settle things for me long-term. Your actions at The Port of Charles Towne have still placed heavy bounties on our heads. Virginia and South Carolina want us dead and I believe that Pennsylvania and Marylandia will soon join in!"

"No matter." Blackbeard smiled.

"No matter? How can you say this???"

"It is of no importance because I have plans to have our names pardoned from Governor Eden himself. Once cleared, it will be illegal for those forces to harass us in North Carolina waters."

"I am still listening, Blackbeard." Bonnet was both interested and sarcastically skeptical.

"We can bask in the peace of The North Carolina Outer Banks safely and snare everything that enters our waters. We will become rich many times over. And this is only the tip of the iceberg."

"And I know that you know Governor Eden personally. I believe he will do this for you but how am I to be assured that I am covered in such pardons?"

"I will stay behind with the crew and see that The Queen Anne's Revenge has been properly cleaned. Her ailments are my fault. I will let you speak with the governor yourself. You can hear it with your own two eyes. I need your trust going forward." Blackbeard stuck his hand out and Bonnet shook it with a slight hesitation.

* * * * * * * * *

June 10th 1718. The land was beautiful and I knew I was near home. Maybe not around the corner from home yet, but we were in The North Carolina seas. I cannot place what was so distinct about it but so be it the salt, the winds or the beautiful lemongrass, I knew I had *not been closer in a year. It felt amazing.*

As we started to navigate the intricate avenue of islands, we were very careful to steer as clear of things as possible. North Carolina's coast had claimed hundreds of seasoned sailors and we would not be next. Surprisingly, Blackbeard gave orders for us to swing right and to the north sharply from our location. What was also surprising was the reaction of the other captains on their own ships. Ambera & Anne-Catherine fell back into a canal out of site. William Lee Graddy followed them without hesitation. We plowed to an area where I could see the surface of the water changing as well as its color. It appeared to be far too shallow to navigate safely but everyone seemed to move on calmly as if they knew what they were doing. I looked behind us and Captain Hands was following us in his own craft.

Stede Bonnet charged forward without ever looking back and we all knew why. He was sitting atop a load of gold, silver, and other booty and more importantly, he wanted his pardon. Safety was paramount to him. If we struggled, it was not important to him. He would be ashore whenever we arrived. Then . . . it happened.

The mighty Queen Anne's Revenge began to rumble and shake violently. I could not sit by silently any longer. Blackbeard remained calm and stood as still as an oak while she reacted below our feet.

"What the hell are we doing??? She's running aground, Sir! We have got to do something quickly!!!"

"Relax Laddy, I know what I am doing. It is now low tide. We are scraping her bottom and cleaning off the rubbish that has attached itself. Just look."

He pointed to the back of the boat and I ran to look. There were trails of seaweed that appeared to be twenty and thirty feet long that was now floating behind us. The vibrations continued and further behind us, Captain Hands still approached. Blackbeard gracefully walked up behind me.

"You see Eli, this will all soon be over. The tide will rise and we will be gone. Do not worry." He then turned to several men standing nearby that looked just as confused. "Gentlemen, ready the dinghies."

"The dinghies? Why Sir? Am I to not understand any of this? What is happening here?"

"You have become an important piece of my story. Of course, you are to understand. But you joined us not only to write but for a sense of adventure. There would be no fun in telling you everything, Laddy." He released a *loud bit of laughter.*

As I looked back, I could see that our sister ship in tow was also running aground although not suffering nearly as bad as we were. Then suddenly, there was a loud snap and The Queen Anne's Revenge came to an abrupt stop. Everyone was thrown forward except for Blackbeard who had seemingly braced himself for what he knew was coming.

Planks from the decking began to lift and the sea came gushing up from under our feet. One of the giant masts over our heads cracked and like a tall, Carolina Pine; it came crashing down amongst us. Our large sails blanketed the crew at the front of the ship as it began to tilt to one side. Finally, he showed excitement in his emotions but even then, he smiled.

"It is time to go, Laddy! Hit the dinghy now!!!" He ran to the edge and jumped over swiftly. I was stunned but quickly followed. Leland and Robin Hood were already there waiting for us. As we landed inside, they quickly began to paddle us away from the dying monster. She continued to scream, crack, and burst slowly from the inside and finally laid completely on her starboard as a few remaining crew members held on and screamed in our direction.

"*Sir? What of the crew left behind? Will The Adventure retrieve them?*"

"*No Laddy, they were not with us at heart and therefore, another choice has been chosen for them.*"

"*They'll die then?*"

"*No, they can easily make it to those banks over there. Bonnet will retrieve them from there and they can join him when he returns to our wreckage.*"

"*Why have you done this? Are you insane? He has all of our booty?*"

"*Does he?*" Blackbeard smiled down on me once more.

"*Yes, I saw them load the trunks aboard his vessel.*"

"*Laddy, I do not know if you have ever seen a magician perform. They have a trick, it's a sleight of hand really. They place a nut on a table for all to see. Slowly, they place a cup over the nut and then slide the cup in line with two others.*"

"*Yes, I have seen such. Please continue.*"

"One by one, they begin to move the three cups in a braiding motion, in and out of each other. Your eyes fixate and try to keep track of the cup in which holds the nut."

"Yes! Yes! I know it well! So you are to tell me that with the motion of the different ships today, you have hidden the nut???"

"All I am telling you is that I learned of a plan that Bonnet had to betray me weeks ago in The Charles Towne Port."

"Really?"

"Yes. And the nut is something he will never find."

"Well then, where is it?"

His smile was much darker this time. "That is something that only The Devil and I know."

* * * * * * * * *

We sat in the corner of Ferrell's Tavern sipping rum. The setting was much different than that of the first *time I had entered. There were no pirates at port tonight other than us. A couple of men sat up front at the bar and one seemed to be enjoying some shellfish.*

I watched Blackbeard and his hands shook. He'd not eaten anything of sorts in several days to my knowledge. When arguing with Bonnet earlier this week, I had seen him use both opiates and coca. I waited for it to start again tonight. When it happened, I would let him know my thoughts without holding back.

Daniel Ferrell came over and sat with us and he had a purpose in his walk when he came over. He and his brother John were friends to piracy and very close friends to Teach. They would do anything for him and that included help him with the information of the day. Today would be no different.

"Well Edward, Blackbeard has become the talk of the world. I'm sure you know this."

"Yes, I do. And I am proud of that."

"You have pulled off some really insane feats my friend. You have attacked the British Navy, held the entire Port of Charles Towne hostage, burned an entire flotilla, you completely rampaged both Spanish Florida & French Louisiana . . . shall I go on?"

"Sure, I enjoy hearing how these activities have been reflected here in The Colonies."

"Edward, do not get me started on the colonies! You had better keep your arse here in North Carolina! You sent a personal message to the governor of Virginia in threats!"

"I was having an emotional day." His smile was as slick as silk.

"Well, you need to make plans to stay on the banks for a while. A Boston publication has as many as fifty ships hunting you . . . and then, you do all of this just to let a second-rate pirate like Stede Bonnet make off with your take? I am astounded."

"Anyone that believes Bonnet could swindle me should feel astounded."

"Then why would he say such?"

"Because at the time, he believed he did."

"Yes, he did. He tore out of Bath Towne in a hurry to run from you and hopefully lose you."

"Do I look like I am in any sort of chase?"

"Well . . . no. So what happened?"

"He believes that he has my gold. Therefore, he ran. That idiot never once thought to check the contents of the trunks. He is of no concern to me and I doubt he will make it three months before he has either sank his ship, been captured, or been killed by his own crew."

"Well, he certainly thinks that you will be in pursuit. He left here with a pardon in hand and even changed his name. That's a bit of information that I am not supposed to be aware of."

"Pray tell."

"Oh yes. He is now known as Captain Thomas and is sailing his ship, The Royal James. He believes that he needs to distance himself from you as well as everything that you have committed. He left here like a scared child."

"Well, he has nothing to fear in me. Despite his best attempt, he has taken nothing from me but an education. Hopefully, he will apply it well."

John Ferrell waved his brother back over to the bar

as several more men came in. He would need his help for at least the next few minutes. Now, Blackbeard smiled at knowing the fate of Bonnet and he slid back in his seat seeking relaxation. From his pocket, he produced several items in which he placed on the table. His pipe, tobacco, a flask of rum, coca leaves and his opiate oils were all there and I became instantly angered.

"What the hell are you doing you, idiot?!"

He smiled and ignored the fact that I was even there. He packed his tobacco into his pipe and doused it with the oils. Just as quickly, he had lit it and took in a large puff in which he held forever. While the dangerous cloud was still inside, he stuffed his jaw with coca leaves and then blew the smoke in my face.

"You are an idiot!!!" Before I could finish any sort of thought, his large hand had wrapped itself around my throat tightly. He held me in place and grabbed his rum. After a brief swig, he spat it in my face and then released his hold on me.

"Laddy, I told you before that I would kill you if you ever cross me. . . "

"You cannot kill anyone. You do not serve your own interests. You serve The Devil! You are his slave;

nothing more!"

"Laddy, you have been good to me but do not think for one moment that I would not leave you here. We are in Bath Towne; your home and I could expose you now and send you back to your little pathetic life. I would not think twice of it."

"You think my life prior to you to be pathetic? Well, it shows how little you know of me. It was often times uneventful but there were people that loved me. Do you have anyone that loves you? Wait! Before you answer . . . you do. Me! I have tried to love you every day. I helped you beat The Devil's Illness and now you spit in my face both figuratively and literally!"

"You do not love me. I am simply all that you have known."

"No, this is not true. I have known people like you. They live right here in Bath Towne. There is a girl here of my own age. I tried to be her friend. I did everything right that a friend would do but she would not accept my friendship. Her family has money and therefore, she has money. She is beautiful, curvy and adored . . . therefore, all men want her hand. But she has no soul. You two belong together."

"Curvy? Adored? Money? Well, I would like to meet her. Perhaps she would become my next bride. Do tell me her name." He knew that pretending to show interest in her would only infuriate me further.

"Ugh, you disgust me. Her name is Mary Ormond if you must know. But let me tell you, she would not do with your unfit life. She would not tolerate your constant drinking and usage of opi. That I promise. And if you try your little marriage trick where the crew rapes her afterward, you would be hung right here by the waterfront. Her family is very well thought of . . . not like you!"

"Oh Laddy, you poor, confused soul. I am Blackbeard and I do as I please. I live as I please and no one will ever change that. No governor, no Navy, no wife . . . and no skinny hermaphrodite, he-she like yourself. This I promise."

"Then go, go find you a wife here of class, riches even! You will see what happens when you pull your stunt. We will test The Devil's Promise to you. Let us see you paddle your little dinghy away as they give chase. You have nothing left. You have nothing! You are nothing!"

"I may be nothing to you but . . . I am all you have."

I stood up and could bear no more. I went to the door and thought for a minute. Walking away from him now could change my entire life. Still, though, I could take no more. He hated me for some reason and always would.

"No! That is where you are wrong! I have a home. You are not my world. You are no more than dog shite, less than even! Between a life of your punishment and my pathetic home . . . I choose home!"

Happily Ever After

I stood at my own front door awkwardly. I was nervous. Would I be accepted back warmly? Had they disowned me? Did they move on easily without me? Do I knock or just walk in? I am not sure this is my home anymore or if I even belong here.

I jumped!!! The dog came up from behind me and licked my hand. At least he remembered me. He gave me the sense of belonging that I was looking for. I turned the doorknob and walked in.

I could hear my mother in the kitchen. The clanging of silverware being placed back in the drawer. There was another bump in the back of the house. Perhaps my brother or father was moving or rearranging something. I walked into the kitchen entrance.

"Mother? I'm home."

"Elizabeth!!!! Oh, my heavens!!! Joseph!!! Matthew!!! Elizabeth is home!!!" Her eyes swelled

instantly, as did my own. She grabbed me in an embrace that I truly felt that I would never feel again. I cried so hard and I could never imagine that home could have felt this good.

My father and brother came running into the kitchen as would a bolt of lightning. The questions were abundant as you can only imagine. "Where have you been? Are you well? Why did you leave? Are you here to stay? When did you arrive home?" They never ended and I could not possibly keep up with the pace at which they were being tossed.

"Wait, wait everyone. Come sit down. I will answer all of your questions." Everyone pulled up a chair at the kitchen table and stared like a group of children awaiting ghost tales.

"So, I did not tell anyone of my opportunity because I feared you would try to stop me. As you know, I love books, writing, reading, and all that goes with such as a whole."

"Yes but . . ."

"Mom. Stop. I will answer everything." She calmed herself as best possible.

"I have also always loved reading about piracy and privateering. One day while on a walk, I found a hat that I knew had to belong to one of them. It was on the road in front of Ferrell's Tavern."

"Ferrell's Tavern??? Elizabeth!!!"

"Mother. Rest please." Once more, she did but seemed to be a boiling pot in danger of running over.

"So, once inside of Ferrell's Tavern, I realized that many of these men were just as wild and rambunctious as the stories told, but also, many were not. They were intelligent and well-educated gentlemen."

"So, in speaking to them, I learned that Captain Hornigold was in need of a scribe. I had an opportunity to see the world, write about the things that I love, and get paid for it."

"But it is so dangerous!!!"

"Mother . . . "

"Sorry."

"So I posed as a boy because as we all know, things are just less risky for boys."

"Well, that answers my next question about your attire . . ."

"Mother. Shhhhhhhhh. So that was that. I snuck out the next day and we hit the high seas. I documented his logs and kept them up to date, I sent off writings for multiple gazettes and have been published all over the world!!!"

"That is so exciting, Dear! So we heard that Hornigold was now a pirate hunter. Are you with him still? Does he treat you well?"

"I have actually not seen or heard from him in months other than a couple of correspondences. Upon his retirement, I went with Blackbeard."

My father banged his fist on the table. "You have been with Blackbeard???"

"Father, I named him."

"Are you lunacy-stricken??? Have you seen the things that they are writing about him???"

I stared at him for a moment. "Father, think of your question. Most likely, you are reading my words *relayed. He wants to be seen as fearsome, he wants to be hated. This is the duty I am charged with. I make him this way."*

"So you are in no danger? He is a gentleman? Like Bonnet? I have also learned that he and Bonnet tried to hornswoggle each other. What have it?"

"Yes, both tried to dupe the other but only Teach was successful. Now . . . as for being a gentleman, I would not go so far. But he has been very good to me."

My mother grabbed my hand and had a twinkle in her eye. "Elizabeth, you have been all over the world and have met people from everywhere. Have you found love?"

"Mother, only you. Yes and no. I have found a man that I absolutely adore but he is much older, very busy and has no interest in me."

"No one else?"

"No, no one else. Perhaps it is not time for me to love or at least, not the time for anyone to love me."

My dad interjected with much more calmness this time. "Elizabeth, I say all of this sincerely. I am very proud of you and all that you have done. What has happened with Blackbeard? Is he here in Bath Towne? Are you going back to sea with him?"

"He is here, father. For how long, I do not know. I am supposed to meet with him today. I know not of his future plans. I am not even sure if he knows."

* * * * * * * * *

I spent part of the day out working with my mother in the yard. It was never my favorite thing to do but it was a chance to spend time with her. I also went fishing with my father and brother and we luckily brought in quite the haul for supper. I did not know what would happen with Blackbeard and my career but I did know that if he would take me back today, I would come running.

I loved my home and my family but in only hours, my world becomes small once again. I caught myself staring at the water off and on. I also kept watching to see if he in some way was trying to leave me. I had no meeting set up with him and had no idea if he was still at the tavern but I would soon try to find him.

Eventually, curiosity got the best of me and I took off walking to Ferrell's Tavern. I could still remember the

nervousness that I had the last time that I made this walk.
I also remember meeting Mary Ormond along the way.
This also reminded me that I was no longer dressed the
part of a cabin boy. I was unsure if they would even allow
me in the door. This was not a place for me.

As I approached, I could smell the strong aroma of
fish. Off to the side, I saw Leland. He was cleaning his
catch. I approached although I knew that I would most
likely not get an answer that I could decipher.

Then, I caught myself. Would he recognize me and
if so, was that a good thing? I thought again about
engaging with him and then backed off. He glanced up at
me and saw a skinny girl in a dress, then looked back
down. He was without a clue.

I pushed the door open and went inside. Even
during the day, it was dark. I recognized no one other
than John Ferrell. He looked up and had the look that he
felt I may be lost. I was not too sure he would even
recognize me. I was correct.

"Ma'am, can I help you? I do not see it fit that you
would be here."

"Yes, yes Sir. I hope that you can. I was told that
Edward Teach would be here. I need to see him."

"Teach? What do you need with him?"

"Well, I have business with him. Now, I know that you find this odd but I have traveled here to relay a message to him. It is one of great importance from the governor. It could mean a lot to him and his financial future."

"Well, that seems peculiar that the governor would send a child."

"I am no child. I am twenty-two years old, thank you very much."

"I meant not to offend, Dear. However, you are in luck, regardless of your message."

I looked at him harshly. "Why is that?"

John looked at me and snickered. "Well ma'am, he is with the governor as we speak. My brother Daniel took him via horseback this morning. They were all in good spirits."

"They?"

"Yes, they. Edward met a gentleman here last

night that proposed many different interesting business dealings. I do believe that he even intends to marry his daughter. Teach did not want to settle down and start a legitimate business here in town without obtaining his pardon first. I cannot blame him for such. There are quite a few papers on his head right now. You must know this if you represent the governor."

"Yes, yes of course I did but who is this lady that he seeks to marry. I have heard nothing of it!"

"William Ormand's daughter. He owns thousands of acres just west of here."

"Yes! I know him well but you cannot be referring to Mary! She is his only daughter that I am aware of!"

"Most likely then. I do not know her personally. I simply know that Teach is going to privateer The Pamlicoe for Mr. Ormond, move products, keep things safe, and so on."

"Outrageous!!!" With the manner that I stomped away, he would surely relay my visit to Blackbeard. But the question is if he would even understand who the irate young lady was that asked of him. He was brilliant. I am sure that he would.

* * * * * * * * *

*Three days passed by and nothing. There was no
sign or word of him. I often looked out of my window at
the bay. The water was beautiful and I missed it. Our
little town was growing. In my absence, several homes
were built and many more in planning. The horizon was
changing from my small, bedroom view.*

*It gave me a chance to pick up some of the books
that I had left behind and I did so to keep my mind free
from him. It killed me to know that he would marry the
one person in the world that I hated. Would he pull some
devilish trick on her as I had seen him do so many times
before to so many unsuspecting maidens? Or worse, would
he settle down with her, have children and raise a family
right here in Bath Towne where I would have to watch?
There was no good answer for me. My mother knew
something was wrong but she let me be to my ways. This
was odd for her.*

*Like a slap in the face, I saw him! I could not
believe my eyes. There I sat on my bed and noticed
movement from the corner of my eye. It was nothing
unusual. There had been people moving about all day with
the new houses between our home and the water. People
were showing interest in them by droves.*

He stood there, dressed in an all-black suit. No less, one that I probably bought for him. His arm was wrapped tightly around Mary as he held her close to him. No doubt, he had not chosen to deflower her yet.

Several men stood with them and walked them around the home. He was going to be my neighbor. This was something that I was not prepared for. I wanted to find a way to stop it but had no idea how. I sniffled and this reminded me that I had started crying once more. I rethought my whole life and would never understand what I had done to deserve this.

I could not stand it any longer. I threw my book to the floor and stomped out of the house. I started to leave the porch and then thought for a moment. I wonder if he has told her of me. I wonder if she knew my feelings for him. I would play a reserved role in secrecy until I knew more.

As I approached, they all turned to see me coming. I introduced myself to him. "Hello good Sir, I am Elizabeth Ellis. It appears we will be neighbors." He looked me over with his devilish smile and winked at me as he kissed my hand.

Mary interrupted. "Edward, this is Elizabeth. We

are childhood acquaintances."

He smiled. "So, she is a friend of yours?"

Mary gritted her teeth. "She's an acquaintance."

I smiled as if her sarcasm had escaped me. I could tell that she knew nothing. I could tell that she knew nothing of the fact that I had saved his life, given him his name; bathed his naked body during sickness.

I remained polite. "Yes, I saw that I was going to have new neighbors and wanted to welcome you both. I hope that if you need anything in getting settled, you will gladly let me know."

She seemed put off. "Well, I do not see why we would need you for anything, Elizabeth. We are to be married tomorrow and Edward has done well for himself. He has promised that we will have a slave or two in place to care for any needs that should arrive."

"Now that sounds splendid, Mary but know that I am here. And for heaven's sake, should you change your mind and desire to employ someone you know and not bring a stranger into your home, please let me know."

He quickly stepped forward as to cut the

conversation off. "I find that to be an excellent idea. If you can cook and clean, I would feel much more comfortable with you in our home rather than purchasing a negro."

Mary grimaced once more. "I suppose that would be fitting. Our home is simple and quaint . . . and to my knowledge, there are not any other slaves down at this end of Bath Towne."

She dropped her tissue and bent over to get it. As she did, her large breasts nearly fell out from the top of her dress and it only served as a reminder of why I could never have what it was that I really wanted.

Blackbeard shook my hand once more. "It was so incredibly nice meeting you Elizabeth. I hope that you can start by Friday. We are to be wed tomorrow with Governor Eden, no less, presiding over our sacred day. I hope that you will be there?"

I smiled up at him. "I would not dare miss it.

* * * * * * * * *

The big day was here. As I neared the outdoor setting, everything was beautiful. How could it be that they would be wed as royalty? Mary's father was beyond rich, but this was more. His status in this part of the countryside was astonishing. I had never witnessed such a celebrity presence. This was a beehive of aristocrats. All thought that they were more important than the next.

As the wedding proceeded, I thought about the moment that Governor Eden would ask the crowd for objections. He's a rapist. He's a satanist. He's a sadist. He's an addict. No, the more that I thought about the situation, the more I knew that this was what Mary deserved. And yet, I would gladly trade with her at any time. Should she not play her role well, I would slip into her bed as often as possible and replace her.

****

I knocked on their door. It was silly to do so I suppose. Immediately after the wedding, Edward asked me to go ahead to their home and make sure that everything was prepared for their first night. I was honestly surprised that he would want me there; being alone with his maiden would be more important, one would think.

Regardless of the situation or why, he wanted me there. He always wanted me by his side. This was calming for me. Be it to punish me or not, he always found a way *to have me there. This alone gave me the most pathetic of hopes.*

I went inside. The home was nice, small actually but very nice and neat. All homes were this way I should think. It smelled of cedar and candles. It was cozy. I found some cutlery and china that needed to be put away in the kitchen, I did so and then made my way to the bedroom.

The bed frame was ornate and huge. It was a heavy-made wooden frame and sat very high. She had a vanity area that I am sure mirrored what a queen might have. The Queen of Bath Towne . . . I am sure this is how she found herself.

On the floor, they had a couple of trunks and other personal effects that they had not had the time to properly put away as of yet. I opened each one and made sure that the contents of each too found a suitable home. The place was so new, there was not much else to do.

I looked out the window to make sure that they were not on their way back yet; they were not. I quickly slid my dress down to my ankles as well as my undergarment and stood there naked.

I brushed my hand over the fabric that covered the bed. I had never felt anything so soft and so fitting for The

Queen of Bath Towne. I am sure that the home of every attendee there today had some just as elegant.

I laid down on top of it and it felt so good against my skin. For a minute, I could have been royalty also. It felt amazing to me in every place it made contact and it also elated me that my naked body would move around these beautiful beddings before hers would. I was a dog amid a territorial pissing.

****

A sharp knock woke me from my accidental slumber. Someone was at the door. As I lifted my head, I realized that I had been caught. Both stood in the bedroom doorway looking at me and both shined with an entirely different emotion.

Mary had a look of disgust on her face but also of reservation. He had apparently told her to say nothing. She followed orders strictly. He smiled like the sadist he was.

"Elizabeth, Elizabeth, Elizabeth, do not cover yourself now." I quickly scrambled to find my dress. Then, he spoke more loudly and less playfully. "I said to NOT find your clothing and that is what I meant."

I froze sitting away from them both. As he directed me to not dress, Mary stared at him in awe. "Stand up, Dear Elizabeth. Face us." Slowly, I did.

"So, you pretend to have carnal relations here in our very bedding?"

"No! No Sir, I would never. I fell asleep after doing the work you asked and . . ."

"Shut up. Anything I ask of you is rhetorical. Your words have no importance to me. Now we must ask, how would one punish such an offense? And on the first day of employment? Such a most serious offense."

"I'll go . . ."

"No, you will stay. Look, Mary, look at her muff. She is so skinny, it nearly spans from hip to hip. How odd."

All I could think is that this was not the first time he had seen me undressed. He was simply using this as a chance to humiliate me.

"Mary, have you ever seen such a body?"

"No Edward, I have not."

"You would think that there is no food to be had here in Bath Towne . . . but then, there is your beautiful body to remind me otherwise. Show her your body."

Mary turned white as a ghost and paused in her thoughts of embarrassing me. He looked down at her with no smile and we both saw that he was serious. She did the same. We stood there facing each other, both near tears.

"Now Elizabeth . . . this is the type body that belongs in such fine bedding. Do you not agree?"

"Yes Sir, she is beautiful."

"That, she is. So here is how we will punish you. You will go sit at the vanity and you will look back at us in the mirror while I make love to Mary. Then you will know what it is like."

Mary and I answered in tandem. "No!"

He quickly took Mary by the arm and slung her to the bed in a way that was somewhere between playful dominance and pure hate. He then went over to the vanity and slid the chair out. Much more gently, he took me by the hand and led me over. I sat without moving. I could *see Mary looking at me in the mirror's reflection.*

He stood behind me and our gazes met in the mirror. He slid his jacket off, then his boots and trousers. Finally, his shirt and hat hit the floor and he stood behind me naked. He placed his hands on my shoulders and massaged my neck, ran his fingers through my hair, and then bent down and kissed me atop the head.

"Each night, you will come to sit at the vanity while I make love to my wife. You will be reminded of what you would have if you had come from a nicer family, if you had a better body, and if you were . . . to be quite honest, prettier."

I could see Mary wiping her tears. He turned to face her. As he bent over and kissed her tummy and breasts, she pulled at the bedsheets in which I had just laid. Then he moved forward, breaking my heart and hers. A little part of us died together that evening.

Kill And Be Killed

August 19th, 1718. I have decided to pick the quill back up at his request in an official manner for him. His day trips under the service of Mary's father and the governor have now grown longer and longer. They stretch out for three, four, and five days. It destroys Mary that I am by his side at each and that she is never even allowed aboard The Adventure.

His runs have also become much more than just that of his employers' bidding. On at least two different occasions, he has pirated vessels of both French and Spanish makings. Governor Eden received notice that Blackbeard was now wanted in all colonies other than North Carolina and that his seat could be questioned if he continued to support or harbor him.

This was of no importance to Eden. He had directly stated that no other colony would have the audacity to come on his sovereign grounds to extradite anyone. From a legal standpoint, Eden was correct. His signature was a direct representation of The Crown in which the colony had ruled. Still, though, the rumors were vast that multiple warships were at rest far off the coast in wait.

No amount of political pressure would change The Governor's mind or the mind of William Ormond for that fact. As gruesome as a problem that Blackbeard was, he was privateering stolen goods to them at a breakneck pace and they only grew richer. On some level, if not many, I am sure that Mr. Ormond loved his only daughter dearly but he was also willing to be quite tolerable of Mr. Teach and his ways due to the facts of business.

Her father had no idea that every night, I was asked to undress and watch Edward make miserable love to his daughter. Such debauchery would be criminal if it were anyone else. Yet at The Port of Bath Towne, it was commonplace.

Through everything, he kept me by his side. The things that we were doing asea would have instantly revoked his Royal Pardon, but he trusted me. The things that I knew he was capable of would ruin his name and marriage, but he kept me in their home. Demented as it was, I knew he loved me. I also knew that he did not love her. More satisfying was, she knew this as well.

She began to question him more and more about

his business as well as the long stints that we stayed out. If feeling polite, he would explain that it was business, and none of hers. If feeling more volatile, he would become belligerent and threaten her life.

Then, about a week ago, she discovered his usage of coca and opiates. Upon her questioning of this, he told her that if she continued to try to run his life, he would kill her father. He said so many hateful things to her, all of which I witnessed. Through them all, she never failed to tell him that she loved him. Never once did he ever say it to her.

The relationship between she and I was strained at best. I had never liked her and she had no respect for me. This had not changed. However, through her nightly sessions in which I watched, I think she felt that she needed to have a conversation with me. One night, it finally happened.

She demanded to know the full nature of the relationship between Blackbeard and I. She believed it to be very sexual. She believed that when asea, I was his whore. She thought me to be a concubine. I assured her that I was not. She still had no idea about our pasts.

On a second occasion, she came to me in a much more broken fashion. He had forced her to smoke an opiate cocktail and she feared one day, becoming the same as he.

She must have truly been at her wit's end because she wanted to kill him. She had thought it through and even devised a plan. What was more evident in her desperation was the fact that with all of this, she trusted me.

"Mary, I know that we have had our lifelong differences and I do not see this ending anytime soon but I need you to trust me. You cannot kill him."

"Why??? Because you love him? You have been with him haven't you?"

"No. You are entirely missing what I am saying. I am telling you that he cannot die."

"Why? Because of my father? The governor? I do not care about the arrangements anymore. They mean nothing. I must be rid of him."

"No. What I am about to say to you is far bigger than any arrangement. Blackbeard, Edward Teach . . . cannot die. He cannot be killed. He has Satan's protection. He has made a pact with The Devil."

"Elizabeth??? Are you insane? Why would you

think this? If this is actually true, and I am not saying that I believe it, but how would you even know?"

"I cannot tell you how I know. All that I can say to you is that I know it to be fact. I witnessed this first hand. He is a god walking among us."

"I only serve one God, Elizabeth Ellis and he is not it!"

"That is where you are wrong. He is a god and I have seen you serve him over and over again."

"Well he believes himself to be all powerful, but he is not. My family, their wealth, their connection; this is true power. My plan is already underway. All that I ask of you is to not say a word of this."

"Tell me your plan. Have you hired a hatchet to do him in? I warn you now, it will not work. Somehow and in some way, he will learn of it and survive it."

"I have done much better than a simple assassin, I have been in communications with The Governor of Virginia and he has Navy Forces ready to slay him."

"We are in North Carolina and they would never march on our soil. I am so sorry but I know this to be

fact."

"As do I. That is why they will take him asea. I simply need to know his haunts. I need to know where he goes when he leaves here. Only you know these things. So tell me now . . . where is it that he goes."

I hung my head. I did believe in his pact but I did not want to place him in harm's way. The more I thought, the more things that came to mind of his hateful treatment of me. He did not appreciate me or the love I had for him. He forever thought and expressed how ugly I was to him. He made a constant mockery of me. If I did not at least test the strength of his demonic pact, I would live a life of watching him make love to a woman I hated.

"Tell me now, bitch!"

I mumbled. "Ocracoke."

"Ocracoke? Are you joshing me? There is nothing worthy on Ocracoke. I have seen its shores with my own two eyes. There is nothing there and no sensible connection to the mainland. It is a desert ile essentially. Why would he be traveling to Ocracoke?"

At this point, I felt that I had already said too much and yet, I needed to know if he were immortal. "He is fortifying the island."

"So you are serious? Can he be found on Ocracoke? This is great news. It is desolate. The ships can simply slip into a bay one night, unload marines and they can kill him. No one will even know what happened that far out from prying eyes."

"There are two problems with your plan. First, you have already forgotten, he cannot be killed. I cannot express this enough. Secondly, the troops cannot take him on land. He is fortifying the island into some sort of Piratical Kingdom. And no, I am not joshing you. At my last count, there were more than fifty ships there."

"What??? Fifty pirate ships?"

"Yes. All with full crews. He intends to use it as a base. And with a following of that size, they are unbeatable. They could blockade any town or port, they could even march on any city."

"Elizabeth, at this rate, he could become a world power. My god, the man is truly insane."

"If they are to take him, it will have to be at sea. There is no other option. But even then, he is a masterful tactician. And he is sailing The Adventure now. She is

very fast on the open waters. Double that with the fact that he is only sailing a skeleton crew and no cargo. Catching him will be nearly impossible."

"Will you tell me more of this pact he has with Satan? I am not to say that I believe it but if I can do something to counter it, superstitious or not, I will."

"Yes, it is actually quite simple. He is not allowed to kill."

"Ridiculous. He is a stark-raving murderer. He has killed hundreds, maybe thousands."

"No, this is where you are wrong. He has killed no one; ever. He will not. He cannot. He always places himself in a position so that he does not have to."

"How do you know this?"

"I cannot say. All that I can tell you is that it is true and that even if a hundred soldiers board his ship, he will somehow and in some way survive it."

* * * * * * * * *

October 2nd, 1718. I will never forget this day. I

lay sleeping on my side. I had almost forgotten where I was. His hand lightly grabbed my shoulder and shook me to awaken. After forcing himself on her last night, he asked that I lay with them until morning. Of course, I did.

I, sleeping on the outer edge softly rolled off the bed first. He then followed. We were both careful to not wake up his bride. I had no idea why we were up but, always holding true, if he went, I went.

As we stepped down the hall, he pointed to my room and then whispered. "You have five minutes. Gather your things."

"My things? All of them?"

"Yes, gather what is important. Eli is needed, not Elizabeth."

I nodded and did as he asked. When leaving the bedroom, I peeped in on Mary once more and she was still sleeping soundly. I walked to the front of the house and walked outside quietly. He was there, already smoking one of his mixtures.

"I wish so badly that you would not do that."

"If I wanted a wife, I would not be leaving

mine.""So, we are truly leaving? We are out to sea for good?"

"We are headed to My Kingdom."

I thought to myself as he spoke. 'His Kingdom? He truly does believe himself to be a god.'

We hurried quickly to the ship. Instead of resting in The Bath Towne Port, our limited crew had already brought it up to a small pier within a two-minute walk from our home. I could see The Adventure from the yard.

As the finishing preparations were readied, a foreign voice echoed over the deck and across the water. It was Mary and she was irate.

"You conniving son of a bitch! You were to just leave me at home without even saying Goodbye?" Then, her eyes locked on the fact that his baggage was packed and present, as was my own. "You were going to leave me permanently? You are a coward! Do not worry! I am glad to be rid of you! Do not ever come back!"

He smiled and slowly walked in her direction. There were not many crew members onboard, but there was still enough for his sadistic idea. One by one as he walked by his men, he playfully tossed them a coin. They knew what this meant. In single file, they went down the narrow steps into the cabin.

She stared at him as if it may be her last moments and I myself feared for her. She had no idea what was about to happen. He removed his cutlass and placed it under the shoulder of her garment. It was razor sharp and passed right through. As it fell loosely, it nearly exposed her breast on that side but she quickly crossed her arms.

He grabbed her by the arm and walked her to the edge of the stairway. "Ok gentlemen, I have something special for you this early morning! The little furry, fancy article between this whore's legs is one of class and distinction!" With one swift shove, he tossed her down below and her screams began.

I listened to her pain, humiliation, and agony for four or five minutes. Then Edward bobbled his head over the cabin opening and gave them playful directions. "Ok gentlemen, I need you to finish your ways with the bitch. We have a long day of sailing ahead!"

Within moments, they were climbing out and going to their stations to finish any preps that were needed. Then, her hand came over the edge and she pulled herself up. Although still clinging, her dress was barely of use anymore. If she had nothing else, she still had her fire and bravery. Mary approached Teach, slapped him and then uttered a devastating admission. "You fool. I am with child."

He said nothing to her. Finally, he looked over to me and signaled for me to come over. I did but with hesitation. He reached down into his boot and produced a small knife and handed it to me. "Kill her and the bastard child now." I knew that he could not.

I took the knife in one hand and grabbed her arm by the other. I walked her to the edge of the ship. With my back to the audience behind me, I gently cut her side as to not cause serious injury. They could not see what the effects of the blade were. I gave her a wink and then shoved her into the water.

I turned to my crew and playfully demanded. "Ship Ahoy!"

* * * * * * * * *

As we approached, I could not believe the progress of the last week. There is no end to what a crew of a thousand men or more could achieve. There were dozens of walls; buildings large and small. Even from the sea, you could see where paths were being scraped. There were *horses pastured and several docks were beginning to extend out beyond the shore.*

I had been aboard The Adventure as it has made passes by the island more than once but this was the closest I had been and it was astounding.

* * * * * * * * *

November 21st, 1718. As with every night on his island, they were one huge chain of parties in which the world had never seen. He was at home on a ship but had spent most of his time sleeping in hammocks and bunks under tents. I think he had finally found a place that he felt safe.

This night, I noticed something different about Edward. Although he had been drinking mildly, he had used no opiates to my knowledge. I had been close by and not noticed anything. Often found it to be a source for his hateful nature, or at least that was my hopes.

I sat and relaxed. I must admit to enjoying a bit of rum myself on that night. In time, a young lady not more than my own age would come to sit beside me. She did not seem to be there for the same reasons as the others. Quietly, she seemed to want to talk to me directly. I broke the silence.

"So, how are you tonight? My name is Eli Ellis."

"Well hello, Eli. My name is Kristi, Kristi Phelps. Tonight is my first night here and you looked to be about my age, so I came over."

"How did you end up here, Ms. Phelps?"

"My father, he is making a delivery of planks here. We are from Mattercommack Creek, up north."

"Very nice. They have done such a great job here with construction. I have truly never seen anything go up any faster."

"Yes, he truly is a brilliant man, is he not?"

"He? You speak of Blackbeard, I assume?"

"Yes, Blackbeard. Edward Teach. Is he here? I would like to meet him."

Something seemed off. I could not place what it was. The cadence in her words, the message or sincerity of it; I did not know. But now, she was asking if he was there and wanted to know his whereabouts.

"Yes, he is here. He is just over there seated in the corner. But I must warn, he does not take easily to new faces. Stay here, I will go over and speak with him for a moment on your behalf."

I smiled at her and she smiled back. She seemed so friendly and so patient.

**

"Edward, I have a question for you."

"Yes, laddy, what is it?"

"Do you love me?"

"What is the meaning of this?"

"I want to know if you love me. I have done everything I could for you. I have spent all of my short, adult life with you. I hold all of your secrets and I travel the world with you. I am asking, do we ever have a chance together?"

He leaned in. I could see the heaviness in his eyes. He had used opiates. He laughed softly. "Laddy, I find you hideous. You will travel with me for the rest of your life and you will die an ugly, old virgin. Can I make myself any more clear?"

"No Sir. I understand. Thank you for being so honest." I walked back over to the young lady and sat with her.

"You are here to kill him, are you not?"

"What? Why would I kill him? Or kill anyone?"

"Because you referred to him by the name Edward Teach. No publications have referred to him by that name in some time. I have seen sure of it. In fact, before the name Blackbeard was established, he was called everything from Teach, to Thatch, Tiche and really, everything in between."

"But . . ."

"Shut your mouth and listen. I will ask you once more. Realize that I already know your intent and I need your honesty. I will not reveal you. Now listen to me. Are you here to kill him?"

"Yes." One word, that was it. That was all it took. She made her point clear.

"Listen to me closely, whatever your name is. You cannot succeed here on land. Anyone that nears will be approached. I am going to tell him you are an axe, here to kill him. I want you to disappear into the crowd. I will tell him that he needs to sleep on the sloop tonight and that it's safer."

"Why are you helping me?"

"That is of no importance. Now, I am to assume there are Navy ships here and waiting?"

"Yes, but out of security, I will not say where."

I quickly grabbed a stick of carbon from the desk over in the corner and a piece of paper and began sketching. "Take this map, your Naval Commanders will know the location. He will be on board a small sloop tomorrow at dawn. He will be sleeping. It has a crew of six on board including myself. Please let them know that I have helped and that I am on your side. He must be stopped. I will be the one with the quill in my cap. Do you understand?"

"Yes, I understand. And I do not know why, but I trust you. Please do not betray me."

I smiled. "I have no reason to betray you but you better bring every single available man."

"Why? The crew is small and you will not even be fighting, I assume."

"As I said, bring every single available man. Now go."

* * * * * * * * *

I did not sleep a wink. Even on the small sloop, the water was completely calm and there was no wind. While I am sure that the anchor was down, it probably served no purpose. At this rate, any would be attacking warship would never make to us. The stillness of things was eerie.

You could hear the ship squeak and creak, you could hear the occasional fish jump near the boat. You could hear mosquitos that had made their way down below and you could still hear the party going on from far away in the distance.

As if he somehow knew the exact directions of his future attackers, Blackbeard positioned his sloop perfectly. With the shore to his bow and a sandbar to the rear, all approaches would have to come from the right or left. This *allowed for us to fire five guns from each side.*

Just before dawn on the morning of November 22nd, 1718, the silence of the water was broken. The water was so slick and the winds so dead, The Navy had to actually paddle their small ships to reach us. From the right, we released five cannon blasts at the same time and in what was one of the greatest examples of cannon marksmanship that I have ever witnessed, all five shots made contact.

The deck of the boat erupted and the main mast fell into the water. By the time that the next round had been unloaded on it, you could see that it was taking on water and would eventually slip below the surface. It was no longer of danger to us. We quickly shifted to the other side of The Adventure so that we could meet this challenge just as well.

Now, it was a one on one battle and I could easily see how this would go. Somehow and once again, this demon would escape. I could not decide if it made me love him more or hate him more.

We fired! Once again with amazement, all five shots were accurate. After only a moment, half of the deck was destroyed and the front hull was breached. The only luck that our enemy had was that they were at least able to maneuver behind us and out of line for the second round of firing. At this point, it was of little importance.

Our one ship had disabled two. To one side, the navel sloop known as The Ranger had sunk and came to rest on a sandbar. Around it were dozens of bodies floating in the water. To the rear of the boat was the other. We recognized the flag instantly. It was The Jane and it was commanded by Captain Robert Maynard. They were indeed here illegally.

Blackbeard was so happy to have Maynard where he wanted him. This captain had made quite a name for himself as quite a pirate slayer. Now, he would never be a threat again.

The wounded British sloop hobbled behind us. Blackbeard called for the anchors to be dropped and the dinghy readied. I looked at him insanely.

"Sir, we're going to board the British vessel???"

"Yes, we are, now load up. Bring your pistols and sabres, men!!!"

***

As the small craft slid up beside the wounded sloop, we stepped on board with as much ease and caution as possible. The deck was in complete destruction. The sails, flags, and ropes had fallen into a large pile. Items were thrown randomly to the right and left. This ship was a sitting duck. Then, Captain Robert Maynard himself walked out with his hands up.

Blackbeard laughed. "So, the infamous Pirate Slayer, Robert Maynard. How fortuitous for me."

Maynard replied. "I do not know what you wish to do with me but I urge you now, take your men, get back on your boat, and leave. If you kill me, you will never live another day in peace. I am an officer of The British Navy!"

"No, you are an officer that has invaded sovereign waters. You are a war criminal."

"No, this is where your logic is failed. I assure you, if you move forward, you will regret it so."

"Why??? Because you are the one and only, Robert Maynard? Look at you!! You are nothing now. Look down at your flag! It lies there with the rubbish that has become your ship!!!"

What Blackbeard did next would alter the course of history. Maynard's flag had fallen from above and landed atop the wreckage. Blackbeard removed his pistol and aimed it at the flag. While smiling at The British Captain, he fired. When he did so, a man grimaced from underneath. He had hidden there when our team boarded. Teach heard his struggle and quickly yanked the flag back to reveal his victim. The man coughed once more as blood erupted from his mouth like a volcano. Then, he died. Blackbeard had killed.

Captain Maynard quickly drew his pistol and shot Teach in the gut. It did not stop him or even slow him down. Suddenly, British Seaman rushed from below the deck. There must have been thirty or more; maybe quite a bit above that.

I threw my hands in the air instantly, as did the rest of our handful. Teach did not. He charged them and with impact. Before he arrived at their mob, he was probably hit with at least four or five more pistol volleys, but he still charged. With his cutlass swinging from right to left, he jumped into the sea of red coats. I could see one soldier after another raise their sword and then bring it down into his body. He continued to fight.

Men continued to push to get to Blackbeard. I believed that each wanted to be able to tell the tale to their *grandchildren that it was their blade that killed him; it was their blade that had made the seas safe; it was their blade that had killed the devil himself. Finally, Maynard commanded and they all backed away. When they parted, there laid his body. He had been shot, stabbed and slashed over and over. He was unrecognizable. Maynard raised his own sword high and with a swift blow, he decapitated the monster. A single tear ran down my cheek.*

The Devil And I

*A woman scorned. I know, you thought it would be
something more complex, more complicated. I cannot take
complete blame for his downfall. He was a fearless, devil-
worshiping, sadist, megalomania-ridden, drug abusing,
narcissistic rapist. Still though, I do suppose that it was
none of these things that actually caught up with him. In
the end, it truly was the affairs of the heart and treating
people with decency that made his bed.*

*I say all of this with absolutely no malice or
hatred. I stayed mad with him, despised him but make no
mistake; I loved him. He was brilliant; dashing. When he
was driven, he was unstoppable. Take all of the ill will
and push it aside. Any woman will tell you that their
heart can never belong to perfection. We need a chaos that
will stir our emotions. I never loved another man as I did
him.*

*I went on to marry and live a happy life. I had
children, grandchildren and now great-grandchildren. My
only regret to this day was not sharing a night with him*

before his downfall. I suppose the fantasy of what it would have been like was far more capable of living on than what reality would have ever been like. After the day he died, I never mentioned him to another person. I was a forgotten part of his legacy.

Over the last six decades, and for the next six I am sure, the one constant concern for all was finding his treasure. When questioned about it from myself or any other, his answer was always the same. Only The Devil & I know. Well, I was there nearly every day and I saw what there was to be seen. Misdirection is a beautiful tool. I know where his treasure is and I have plainly told you. But... did you find it?

Geographic Reference

Edenton: Edenton or Eden Towne is a small town on the Albermarle Sound and was established in 1712 as "the Towne on Queen Anne's Creek". It was later known as "Ye Towne on Mattercommack Creek" and still later as "the Port of Roanoke". It was renamed "Edenton" and incorporated in 1722 in honor of Governor Charles Eden who had died that year.

Bath: Bath or Bath Towne is a town in Beaufort County, North Carolina, United States. Incorporated in 1705, Bath was North Carolina's first port of entry, located on the Pamlico River near its mouth. It developed a trade in naval stores, furs, and tobacco. Bath is North Carolina's oldest town

Port Of Bath: Port Bath operated from 1716 to the 1790s as one of five regional British-American customs collections districts along the coast of North Carolina in the eighteenth century. Today visitors can experience the state's first town and Bath's 300-year history among its surviving colonial structures and at Historic Bath.

Beaufort: Beaufort is a town in and the county seat of Carteret County, North Carolina. Established in 1709 and incorporated in 1723, Beaufort is the third-oldest town in North Carolina. In June 1718, Blackbeard ran his flagship, the *Queen Anne's Revenge* and his sloop *Adventure aground here.*

Ocracoke: Ocracoke is a village on Ocracoke Island, part of North Carolina's coastal Outer Banks region. The landmark 1823 Ocracoke Lighthouse overlooks the village and Pamlico Sound. Set in an early 1900s house, the Ocracoke Preservation Society Museum traces the island's history. Nearby, the tiny British Cemetery contains the graves of WWII sailors. Silver Lake is dotted with boats, and shops and restaurants line its harbor.

Teach's Hole: This is where he lost his head in a dramatic sea battle with the British Navy led by officer Robert Maynard on November 22, 1718, in which he incurred 5 pistol shots and no less than 27 severe cuts in various parts of his body before being brought down.

The Pamlico Sound: Pamlico Sound in North Carolina in the US is the largest lagoon along the North American East Coast

Cape Hatteras: Cape Hatteras is a thin, broken strand of islands in North Carolina that arch out into the Atlantic Ocean away from the US mainland, then back toward the mainland, creating a series of sheltered islands between the Outer Banks and the mainland

Cape Fear: Cape Fear is a prominent headland jutting into the Atlantic Ocean from Bald Head Island on the coast of North Carolina

Made in United States
Orlando, FL
04 February 2023

29484044R00157